ONE PASS AWAY BOOK TWO

After all these YEARS

MARY J. WILLIAMS

About the Author

Want to know how to motivate yourself to write a book? Have your favorite football team lose the Super Bowl. On the last play. With an interception. The next day I was so depressed I tuned out all media. No TV, no internet, no newspapers—nothing. And I started to write. I'm still writing. As you can see, a little motivation can do wonders. Happy reading everyone.

How to Get in Touch

Please visit me at these sites, sign up for my newsletter or leave a message.

http://www.maryjwilliams.net/home.html
https://www.facebook.com/Mary-J-Williams-1561851657385417
https://twitter.com/maryjwilliams05
https://www.pinterest.com/maryj0675/
https://www.goodreads.com/author/show/5648619.Mary_J_Williams
https://instagram.com/2015romance/

More Books by Mary J. Williams

Table of Contents

Prologue

SEAN McBRIDE WOKE up with a smile on his face. It happened a lot lately. And he thoroughly approved.

He stretched his long, athletic body. Some mornings every inch of him ached. Such was the life of a professional football player. Everything was about preparing for the game. Focus. Concentration. The goal was to be ready for game day.

He had to hold it together for sixty minutes. Pull out a win any way possible. Sacrifice his body to the football Gods and pray he walked away healthy enough to do it all again next week.

Sean dreaded the day after the game. The adrenaline had long ago worn off and he felt all of his thirty years. There were degrees of bad. Sometimes he shuffled to the shower, the aches and pains palpable, but mercifully bearable.

Then there were the bad days. After a day of three-hundred-pound defensive backs using him as their own personal punching bag, he didn't get out of bed—he crawled.

Bruised from top to bottom, his joints creaked and his muscles protested like screeching banshees. Those were the times he wondered why he did it. He could have been a doctor. Or a lawyer. He could have taken his father's advice and gone into the family business. No seventeen-year-old with dreams of glory in the NFL wanted to think about becoming a butcher. But damn. Cutting meat sounded good on those mornings.

This was a good Monday. His body felt lithe—limber. The bruises were there. That was part of his life. However, yesterday had been one of those rare games when every moment fell into place. From the kickoff to the final whistle, the outcome of the game was never in question.

Sean caught every ball thrown his way. He evaded the defense. Fast as the wind. Three touchdowns. One hundred and eighty-two total yards. A damn good day for any wide receiver. He would have had more if Coach Coleman hadn't taken him out of the game in the fourth quarter. With a big lead, there was no reason to risk injury when he wasn't needed.

The after-game celebration moved from the locker room to one of the team's favorite hangouts. Naturally the atmosphere was raucous. Cautiously so.

The Knights were having a stellar season. Ten wins, two losses. Sean and his friends had enough games under their belts to understand how quickly that could turn. Injuries tended to come in bunches. So far, they were healthy. However, that was bound to change. The hope was to get to the playoffs with all their major players on the roster.

After the game, they had a few drinks. Three was Sean's limit these days. A few years ago it was a different story. He would have closed the place down after a win. He and his bed partner of the moment would have moved on to someone's apartment, partying until dawn before going back to her place and fucking like demented rabbits. Then he would go home alone and catch a few hours sleep until it was time to grab a quick shower before heading to the Knights' headquarters to review film from the game.

Those days were over. Sean wasn't a kid anymore, high on his own press clippings and more testosterone than brains. Not that he had settled down completely. He could still party with the best of them. However, he chose his moments—ones that never took place during the season.

Women were another matter. Sean liked sex. Always had. If there were a God, he always would. While his bed partners weren't as varied, they were almost as frequent.

Sean knew players who abstained a few days before the game, saving their *juice*. He wasn't one of them. Sean had plenty of juice, thank you very much. Sex was necessary for a happy and healthy mind. For *his* happy and healthy mind.

A big plus to having sex at night was sex the next morning. It was one of his favorite things. A partner, warm and willing.

The perfect way to start the day.

Speaking of which. Smiling, Sean turned over. His hand reached out, expecting to find a soft, sweet woman. Instead, he found cold sheets. Sitting up, he looked around the room. Like the bed, empty. The bathroom door was open and the light off.

Not bothering to cover up, Sean jumped out of bed. Buck naked, he searched the house. She wasn't in the kitchen. Why would she be? She didn't cook, not even coffee. She was on a first-name basis with half the baristas in Seattle.

Was that it? Would she be back soon with two cups of steaming black caffeine and his favorite muffins? Sean was talking himself into that scenario when he saw the note.

He picked up the paper that had been propped against the lamp by the front door.

Sean.

Thank you for the past few weeks. After years of building it up in my mind, I was worried that it couldn't live up to my expectations. I should have known better. It was everything I had hoped for—and more.

We didn't make any promises. No strings were attached that need to be broken. After all these years, you can finally breathe easy. It's over. We are now friends without the expectation of benefits.

When we see each other, it will be as if it, we, never happened.

Sean read the note. Then read it again.

What the fuck? What was in those drinks?

Sean searched his memory for some kind of clue. The bar. His teammates. Then she was there. They laughed. Everything was smooth and easy. They seemed to be developing a rhythm. In his mind, they were together. Not a man and a woman—a couple.

It sounded good to him. He would have sworn she felt the same. He didn't want another woman. He wanted her. In his arms. In his life.

No expectations? Hell. He woke up with plenty of them, only to find out he was alone. Alone in bed. Alone. Period.

Sean scrubbed a hand over his face. He remembered the way she tasted. The way she melted into his arms. The curves of her luscious body pressed against his. Her sighs. His belief he would never get enough of her.

Crumpling the note into a ball, Sean tossed it across the room. Suddenly he felt every ache. His legs felt like lead. Slowly, he shuffled toward the bathroom. He needed a shower. Long and hot. Determined not to look at the bed, Sean's peripheral vision wouldn't let him off the hook that easily. It captured everything. The rumpled sheet. The pillow still holding the imprint of her head. A slash of red on the floor.

Frowning, Sean picked up the scrap of silk. So small he wondered why she had bothered. The image of her standing in nothing but her heels and the panties popped into his head. Unconsciously, his body tightened with desire.

Right, that was why.

Sean ran the smooth material over his cheek, feeling it catch on his morning stubble. He breathed deeply. He smelled vanilla and spice. Her essence. He would never forget it. As long as he lived, he would be able to close his eyes and conjure up her scent. Her taste.

His eyes popped open. *Friends? Nothing more? Bullshit!*

Keeping the panties in his hand, Sean headed for the shower. This wasn't over. Not by a long shot. It was just the beginning.

Chapter One

RILEY PRESTON KNEW football. It was in her blood. Part of her DNA. When other girls her age were watching videos by their favorite boy band, Riley was studying depth charts and draft projections. Her friends threw their hands up in exasperation when she blew off trips to the mall. She preferred a Saturday afternoon game between Ole Miss and Georgia Tech to giggling over the latest fashions.

Her idea of the perfect outfit was jeans and a baggy Seattle Knights football jersey. The shirt had seen better days. Multiple washings and a run-in with the neighbor's Pomeranian had left it faded and ripped. She had a drawer full of brand new jerseys. Her father ran the team, which meant she had access to all the team merchandise her heart desired.

However, the old one held sentimental value. Her grandfather gave it to her on her twelfth birthday. It was the year after he bought the Seattle Knights. And the year before he died of a massive heart attack.

Douglas Preston made his first million dollars with his hands. He worked three jobs doing manual labor—anything and everything. He cleaned up at construction sites. Shoveled shit at a horse farm. Washed cars on the weekend. He saved every dime until he had enough to buy his first piece of commercial real estate. Then another. Then another.

Douglas was a rich man by the time he turned thirty. He married money. At fifty, his million had become a billion. His wife was a stranger—his son an unbearable snob. He wasn't an idiot. He recognized his mistakes. Making money had taken precedence over everything else. His family would never want for anything, but at what price?

Joy entered his life one spring morning. The birth of his granddaughter, Riley April Preston. She was the light of his life. Every ounce of love and affection he hadn't given his wife and son was heaped on her. He didn't make the mistake of giving her material things. He gave her his time. While her parents following in his footsteps—ignoring their only child—Douglas took her to the zoo. Or a museum. Or they would simply walk around Pioneer Square. However, when it was football season, Sundays were reserved for one thing. Seattle Knights football.

Douglas was a season ticket holder. When she was old enough, he took Riley to every home game. Sometimes they would travel to Denver or San Diego or Chicago. Depending on the Knights' schedule.

Riley learned to read, sitting on her grandfather's lap, going over the roster and team stats. She skipped beside him, holding his hand as he explained the difference between an inside linebacker and a defensive end.

When the team came up for sale, Douglas purchased it, giving Riley a small share of the team. It was always his intention to give her his controlling interest. Someday. The dream was for her to learn at his side. When he was ready to turn over the reins, she would be ready.

Neither Douglas nor Riley could have anticipated the heart attack that ended his life much too soon. There was no warning. After his yearly physical, his doctor had proclaimed Douglas to be as sound as a man in his forties. A week later, he was dead.

Her grandfather's passing was international news. World leaders, business moguls, and the entire Seattle Knights football team attended his funeral. That year they wore black armbands on their uniforms. A tribute on opening day lauded the man who helped turn the franchise from middle of the pack to elite. A perpetual contender.

Publicly, the Preston family mourned Douglas' passing with the proper show of respect. Riley's parents said the right things. Gerald Preston praised his father in one interview after another. Corrine Preston cried daintily whenever Douglas' name was mentioned.

Privately, they practically danced on his grave. All the money and power was now theirs. Gerald no longer had to consult his father over every little matter. Preston Enterprises was his company and he lost no time sweeping out anyone who wasn't on board with his plans.

Riley's mother had never gotten along with her father-in-law. She found him crude. He thought she was a cold fish. They were both right. Corrine enjoyed two things. Shopping and showing off her wealth. How better to do that than to throw the lavish parties Douglas had always frowned upon. Gerald didn't care what she did or with whom she did it as long as she kept his home running smoothly.

Neither considered Riley's feelings. To be honest, she sometimes wondered if her parents remembered they had a child. Her grandfather had been her rock. That foundation of love and support kept her going after he was gone. She was strong because Douglas Preston made her that way. He praised her intelligence—not her beauty. *The world is filled with window dressing*, he would tell her. Looks fade. Brains are forever.

When Douglas Preston died, he left her two things. A sense of her own self-worth, and her love of football. More precisely, her love of football, and the Seattle Knights.

Gerald called the Knights his father's ridiculous vanity project. If it had been up to him, he would have dumped the team as quickly as possible. Douglas' will made it impossible. Gerald was a reluctant placeholder. He controlled the team—made the day to day decisions. But he couldn't sell the team.

Riley inherited a small share of the team. On her twenty-fifth birthday, a few more came to her. When she turned thirty, she would be the majority owner of the Seattle Knights.

It was one of the few times Riley saw her father lose his temper.

"Why didn't anyone tell me the old man was leaving you the team?" Gerald demanded.

Riley wisely refrained from saying, *You were told. You just didn't care enough to pay attention.* Wouldn't that have gone over like a lead balloon? Instead, she bided her time. She was twelve years old. She was too young to have anything to do with the running of the team. However, that didn't mean she was powerless.

Riley watched and waited. Her first move came just after her fifteenth birthday. The team was preparing for the yearly NFL draft. The Knights desperately needed help at wide receiver. Their franchise quarterback, Gaige Benson, was a magician. One of the best in the game. However, he needed help if the team was going to get to the Super Bowl. Right now, Gaige's pinpoint passes were dropped more often than not. They needed someone with sure hands and quick feet.

She didn't think anyone turning pro was good enough. Riley went to her father with the suggestion they trade their pick to a team with an established wide receiver. She had graphs and charts to back her up. She thought she had gotten through to him. Gerald smiled, took the information she had spent hours compiling, and left the room.

Riley was crushed when she found out with the rest of the world that the Knights decided to use their pick on a defensive lineman out of Florida State. He turned out to be a bust. As did the tight end they drafted the next year—against Riley's advice.

Then it happened. The moment that would change her life.

Riley didn't bother with college players until their senior year. If someone caught her eye, she would look up their history, but until they were a potential fit for the Knights, she didn't waste her time.

Two years after their attempt to find a wide receiver, the team was still looking. In October, a senior at Georgia Tech caught her eye. Sean McBride was having the kind of season that had people talking Heisman Trophy and number one draft pick.

Riley didn't think McBride was destined for either accolade. The QB for Ohio State was putting up gawky numbers that tended to get awards glory. However, she was certain he would be an outstanding professional player.

College football was all right. However, for Riley, it was a means to an end. There was no excitement. No passion. As her grandfather liked to say, 'you can't get worked up when you have no horse in the race.' Riley's horse was the Knights. Period. End of story. Until one fateful Saturday afternoon.

Sean McBride was being interviewed after his game-winning touchdown. He looked into the camera and smiled. Riley Preston fell in love for the first time.

Tall, with pitch-black hair, his hazel eyes were filled with laughter. Riley didn't know what the joke was, but she desperately wanted to find out.

It made no sense. She wasn't a girl prone to foolish flights of fancy. Football players were athletes. To be admired? Yes. To be worshiped? Absolutely not. Yet, there it was. No matter how many times she tried to convince herself that off the field, Sean McBride meant nothing to her, the harder she tumbled.

Part of her was horrified. What would her grandfather think? She had never met Sean. Never spoken a word to him. As she scoured the internet for any scrap of information, she told herself it was a crush. Her first—naturally it was hitting her hard.

What she found out about Sean should have sent her screaming in the opposite direction. He was the definition of a manwhore. He played hard—on and off the field. If he didn't have a football in his hands, he had a woman. Never the same one. Blond. Brunette. Redhead. The only things they seemed to have in common were large boobs and beautiful faces.

For the first time in her life, Riley stood in front of the mirror and looked herself over with a critical eye. Her build was average. Not skinny. Not fat. A little above average in height with a good complexion and straight teeth. Her face was...? How could she judge? No one had ever run screaming from the room. Children didn't cower in fear when she walked down the street. As faces went, hers was fine.

Riley sighed. Next to Sean's bevy of beauties, she faded into nothingness. Pulling back the neckline of her shirt, she gave her chest a brutal critique. Well-endowed she wasn't.

What the hell? Riley could almost hear her grandfather. *Didn't I teach you better than this? Brains. If you want that boy, dazzle him with your smarts. False eyelashes. False boobs. You don't want someone who can't see past all the smoke and mirrors.*

"Yes, I do."

Riley wasn't proud of it. But facts were facts. She wanted Sean McBride. It was unrealistic—and completely shallow. She chuckled. *See, they already had something in common.*

One thing was certain. For Sean to notice her, he had to be nearby. The draft was only a few short months away. It was time to set the groundwork. Over the past few years, she had learned something important. Her father would never let the team pick Sean if he thought it was what she wanted.

Between now and May, she had to convince him that the last thing the Seattle Knights needed was Sean McBride.

"WITH THE THIRD pick in the draft, the Seattle Knights choose Sean McBride. Wide receiver. Georgia Tech."

The applause filled the room. Riley didn't join in. She sat stoically while Gerald Preston and Patrick Kramer, the Knights' general manager, shook hands. Her father glanced her way. There was a gleam of satisfaction in his eyes. She didn't react. Inside she danced like a maniac.

This was her doing and no one would ever know.

Her plan had been simple. Get Sean's name in her father's head and make sure he believed Riley didn't want the Knights to have anything to do with him. Subliminal messaging. Some people scoffed at the idea. Not Riley. She was now a firm believer. In April, when she saw the team's shorted draft list, Sean McBride was one of three names.

Gaige Benson and head coach Harry Coleman pushed hard for Sean. Riley wanted to kick them both in the butt. *Shut up. You're going to ruin everything.* Luckily, her opinion held more weight with her father. Riley made her choice clear. Take one of the running backs. It was pathetically easy.

A psychiatrist would have had a field day trying to figure out the deep-seated resentment that brewed in her father. What had she done to earn it? What might have fascinated the shrink even more was the fact that Riley couldn't have cared less. She didn't need, nor want, the love and affection of a man who had been nothing but a sperm donor. The father of her heart was Douglas Preston.

Happy beyond measure, Riley rose. She was about to leave the conference room when Gaige Benson stopped her.

"I don't know how you did it, Riley, but thank you."

"I don't know what you mean."

"Yes, you do." Gaige smiled and kept on walking.

Riley didn't know how Gaige had figured out her involvement. Not that it mattered. He wanted Sean on the team almost as much as she did.

Riley stepped out of the team's headquarters, breathing in the wet, spring air. Sean McBride was coming to Seattle. Suddenly, the future seemed impossibly bright and full of possibilities.

Chapter Two

THREE YEARS LATER

"YOU GREEDY BASTARD." Marcellus Weeks, tight end for the Knights, shook his head in amazement. "No one needs three women at a time."

"It isn't about need," Sean McBride informed him. "They were there. They were willing. What would you have done?"

"Run home to his wife with his tail between his legs," Gaige Benson quipped.

Marcellus threw his used towel at Gaige, missing by three feet.

Picking up the towel, Gaige slung it back, hitting the other man in the face. "And that is why they pay me the big bucks."

"QBs," Marcellus said with good humor. "Arrogant pricks, each and every one."

"The hell with you pussies. I want to hear more about our boy's walk on the wild side."

Sean grinned at Sol Fellows. Before the big linebacker had tied the knot last spring, the two of them had closed down more than one club. It seemed more and more of his buddies were moving past their party days. He didn't begrudge them for their need for home and hearth.

However, he missed the camaraderie. Tossing back shots of Jack and scoping out women was more fun with a group. His posse was dwindling fast.

"Wild side?" Sean said with a shrug, his eyes twinkling. "Hell, son. That was just a slow Wednesday."

"Oh, man. You're killing me." Sol groaned. His wife was eight and a half months pregnant. Sex was not in his foreseeable future. "If there is any justice in the world, your dick will fall off from overuse."

The men exited the locker room. Practice was over and the Knights' facility was almost empty. They headed toward the parking lot, laughing companionably.

"Stamina is my superpower. My dick takes a licking and keeps on ticking."

"I need details." Marcellus clasped his hands in mock pleading. "How much licking are we talking about?"

"They passed me around like an all-day sucker. The blond —"

"Ixnay on the dirty talk." When Sean shot Gaige a confused look, the quarterback motioned with his head. "Innocent ears at twelve o'clock."

The other men turned. Five feet away, Riley Preston leaned against her car. Sweet and friendly, the team considered her their unofficial sister. Growing up with brothers, Sean felt a special connection to the owner's daughter. He liked her goofy charm and big, earnest blue eyes.

"Why didn't you say something sooner?" Seeing Riley's wave, Sean smiled and lifted a hand in greeting. "Do you think she heard anything?" he whispered to Gaige.

"That kid has ears like a bat."

"Maybe she didn't understand what we were talking about."

Gaige almost choked on his laughter. "Jesus, Sean. She's twenty years old and hangs around professional athletes. She may not give them, but she knows what a blow job is."

"Shh," Sean frowned. "What the hell, Benson?"

"Hey, beautiful." Gaige ignored Sean's last comment. He gave Riley a friendly hug. "No classes today?"

13

"I had one this morning. Hi, fellas."

Riley smiled at the men, making sure she didn't single out Sean. From the very beginning, she made a point of keeping her feelings to herself. It would be humiliating if everyone knew how she felt. Loving Sean was hard enough without being the butt of the team's jokes.

The men returned her greeting.

"Are you waiting for your dad?" Sol asked.

Other than Gaige, none of the team knew of her strained parental relationship. Something about the QB made her want to spill her guts. She often confided in him about her father. Her mother. School. However, she didn't mention Sean. Never Sean. That was a line she never crossed.

"My car won't start. I called for a tow truck, but they said it would be about an hour."

"I'll give you a lift." Sean's smile was easy. With no effort, he made Riley's heart beat faster.

"I don't want to put you out."

Riley hoped she sounded sincere. Disabling her car had been easy. Her high school automobile maintenance class had finally come in handy. When the mechanic looked under the hood, the problem would be easily fixed and just as easily explained. Things came loose—on their own. There wouldn't be any reason to suspect subterfuge.

"I like the company." Sean draped a friendly arm around her shoulders. "See you guys tomorrow."

Gaige and the other men watched Sean escort Riley to his midnight blue Ferrari.

"He has no idea?" Marcellus asked incredulously

"Not a clue." Gaige shook his head.

"Amazing." Sol sighed. "Sean was born with babe alert. If there is an interested female within a fifty-mile radius, he can scope them out. He's around Riley all the time. Why can't he see her painfully obvious crush?"

"In Sean's eyes, Riley isn't a woman." Gaige walked toward his car, his teammates at his side. "She's a girl. A little sister."

"She's twenty?"

"Yes," Gaige said.

"Well, shit." Marcellus suddenly felt old. He had been with the Knights for ten years. He had watched Riley grow up. In a blink of the eye, she was a young woman and he was sliding down the back end of his career. Where had the time gone?

"We should be grateful for Sean's blinders." Gaige looked over his shoulder as the blue sports car zipped out of the parking lot. "The day will come when Sean opens his eyes and sees what's right in front of him."

"Train wreck in the making?" Sol wondered.

Gaige's smile didn't quite reach his green eyes. "I don't know. Something tells me one day we're going to find out."

"HOW IS SCHOOL going?"

"Good. I love my classes."

Riley wiped her hands on her jeans. She didn't find herself alone with Sean very often. Manipulating the situation seemed like a good idea at the time. It had been a calculated risk. Gaige might have offered her a ride. If he had, she would have taken it without hesitation. It would have been disappointing, but not the end of the world.

When Sean fell easily into her plans, Riley was thrilled. Riding in his car with plenty of time to talk—it was exactly what she wanted.

Finding something to say was harder than she expected. When she was alone, she carried on long, involved conversations with him. However, those were in her head. She was witty and interesting. She flirted like a pro. Not too slutty. Sexy. In her head, she was amazing at doing sexy.

The reality was another matter. Sean asked about school. She could have mentioned all the parties she went to. Her numerous boyfriends. It would be a lie, but he didn't need to know that. Instead, she told him she loved her classes. *Fascinating, Riley.*

She wanted to slap her forehead. Nerd alert! She knew the kind of women Sean liked. Bookworms need not apply.

15

"It's Friday. Have a hot date lined up?" Sean winked.

"Sure. And I might end the night with a blow job."

Riley wanted the earth to open up and suck her in. Why? With a million things she could have said, she chose that? Sure, it was on her mind. She heard what Sean and the guys said. They didn't think that kind of talk was for her ears. Innocent Riley. God. She didn't know which was worse. The fact that Sean believed she was an inexperienced virgin, or that it was true.

"Riley!"

Sean sounded shocked. Appalled. Riley sat up straight. Maybe this was a good thing. She could deal with a little embarrassment if it meant Sean began looking at her in a different way. She was twenty. He was twenty-five. It was time for her to make her move.

"What do you think I do on my *hot dates*, Sean?" Riley challenged.

"I hadn't thought about it."

She could tell Sean was uncomfortable. He bragged up his sex life with the guys. He probably let loose the dirty talk with his many, many conquests. However, one mention of a blow job and color stained his cheeks.

"I'm surprised you can still blush."

"Me too," Sean mumbled. "You shouldn't talk like that, Riley. It isn't…"

"What, Sean? Ladylike?"

"Riley-like."

Riley wanted to tear her hair out. *Riley-like? What did that mean?*

"I'm not a little girl, Sean. How old was the last woman you…?" Riley was going to say dated. Sean didn't date. He enjoyed and moved on. If she wanted him to think of her as an adult, she needed to use adult language. "The last woman you had sex with?"

"Age is different than experience."

"I have experience." Riley waited for the heavens to open up. When lightning didn't strike her down, she breathed a sigh of relief.

"Bull—"

"Go ahead. Say it," Riley dared him.

"Bullshit."

"See. I didn't collapse in a fit of the vapors. There isn't anything you could say that would shock me, Sean."

"Don't be so sure, little girl." Sean shifted the car into a lower gear before he pulled off the highway. "With all the things I've seen and done, *I* can still be shocked. You have no idea what goes on out in the big bad world. And I would prefer to keep it that way."

Riley felt her heart melt. She was ready to let it go, happy that Sean cared about her. He ruined the moment by calling her little girl and patting her hand. He wasn't a man touching a woman. He was a man placating a child.

Three years. She had been waiting patiently. When Sean was drafted by the Knights, Riley accepted that the age difference would have put him off. She had been seventeen and still in high school. At twenty-two, he had graduated college and had a newly signed NFL contract.

Never shy, Riley had let him know who she was. He liked her. She knew that. She put up with the big brother/little sister vibe because she knew her time would come. If he wanted to fool around with every bimbo that flashed her cleavage his way, so be it.

Riley hated watching how easily Sean's head could be turned. However, she was the only one. His teammates followed his love life with good humor. As long as he showed up for practice and did his job, they didn't care what Sean got up to after hours. The press and the Knights' front office weren't so lenient.

Sean McBride's reputation had arrived in Seattle before he did. He partied hard and played harder. Management gave him a warning after the first fight. It didn't matter that he wasn't to blame. Sean would have walked away when a drunk started flinging insults. He didn't care what anyone said about him. He had heard it all. When the man went after Sean's companion, the trouble started. When he demanded the guy apologize, Sean received a face full of beer for his trouble. Even then, he didn't throw the first punch. Witnesses said the drunk attacked Sean, giving the wide receiver no choice but to defend himself.

A swollen right hand hadn't kept Sean out of that week's game. It was easier to turn a blind eye when your rookie sensation made game winning catches. Harry Coleman told him to tone it down, and Sean agreed. Unfortunately, where Sean partied, trouble followed.

Two more fights during his rookie season had Gerald Preston pushing for Sean's release. The shareholders, including Riley, pointed out that they wouldn't be able to find a replacement with Sean's talent. Gerald tried to push the issue. He had figured out his daughter's role in getting the Knights to draft Sean. Nothing would have made him happier than to kick the cocky bastard off the team and out of town. He believed it would have served him—and Riley—right.

The team was never going to terminate Sean over a few fights. However, they didn't like the negative publicity. When Gaige stepped in, incorporating Sean into his group of friends, the antics died down. The QB became the stabilizing influence needed by a young man suddenly faced with more money and fame than he had ever known.

Riley loved that Sean stopped getting into trouble. If he dropped the never-ending stream of women, she would jump for joy.

Sean drove up to her parents' house, stopping the car by the front door. Riley often thought of moving out. She was in college and most of her friends either lived in the dorm or shared an apartment. Finding a place away from Ambleside Road made sense for a young, single woman. It would have done wonders for her social life to have a roommate closer to her own age.

"I'm thinking of getting a place of my own. Or with a friend."

"Really?" Sean put the car in park. "Why?"

"Because I'm twenty. And in college."

"I guess you are." Sean laughed. "When did you go and grow up on me?"

"I swear, if you pat my hand again, I will punch you in the mouth."

"Hey," Sean called out when Riley jumped from the car. Using that famous wide receiver speed, he caught her before she could enter the house. "You've been prickly the whole trip. What's wrong?"

"Nothing." She sighed. "Everything."

Riley had to tip her head back. She loved how tall he was. She loved the way the sun brought out glints of red in his almost black hair. She loved his smile. His hazel eyes. She loved Sean. Period.

"Can I help?"

"Kiss me."

"Sure."

Riley knew it wasn't that easy. Sean aimed for her cheek. A nice, brotherly kiss. *The hell with that.* A second before his mouth made contact, she turned her head. Lips to lips. Finally. Before he could react, she threw her arms around his waist and held on for dear life.

"Riley!"

She recognized her mother's gasp, but Riley didn't care. Sean tried to pull away as gently as possible. She had no intention of letting him go. Her arms tightened. Her lips opened. Who knew when she would get another chance like this one? Audience be damned, she wanted Sean to kiss her back.

With more force, but not enough to hurt her, Sean disentangled himself.

"I'm sorry."

Breathing hard, Riley opened her arms, ready to tell Sean not to be sorry. She wasn't. She was mortified to find out he wasn't speaking to her.

"I don't blame you, Sean." Football bored her mother to tears. Corrine Preston knew who the Knights' players were because she liked handsome young men. When she batted her eyes at Sean, Riley was mortified. "Riley is immature for her age. I'm sure she mistook your kindness for something else."

"Mrs. Preston—"

"Corrine." Her mother smiled, placing her manicured hand on Sean's chest. "Oh, my." She squeezed, smiling slowly.

This couldn't be happening. Riley felt rooted to the spot. She wanted to run, really she did. However, between the one-sided kiss and her mother's outrageous behavior, Riley didn't know if she would ever be able to move.

"I need to be going." With less care than he showed Riley, Sean removed her mother's hand. "Are you okay?"

After making certain he was speaking to her, Riley nodded.

"I'll see you soon."

Sean sprinted to his car, obviously anxious to leave behind two forms of crazy. A grabby young woman and a would-be Mrs. Robinson.

"Thanks for the ride, Sean," Riley managed to call out before he slammed the door.

Instead of a verbal response, Sean waved from his open car window. He pulled out of the driveway like a man being chased by demons. Glancing at her mother, Riley didn't think the description was too far off.

"That was embarrassing." Corrine practically shoved Riley into the house.

"I agree. You groped my friend. Are you out of your mind?"

"I don't appreciate you speaking to me that way, young lady." Corrine fluffed her hair in the mirror. The house was filled with them. Her mother hated to be more than five feet away from her own image. "And I was the one embarrassed. Throwing yourself at a man is bad enough. What would possess you to kiss Sean McBride?"

"How do you know *he* didn't initiate the kiss?"

Corrine didn't laugh. Riley would have preferred it to the look of abject pity.

"A man like that is out of your league."

"You think he's in yours?"

"I could have him in a second." Corrine's lips curved into a knowing smile. "If I weren't a married woman."

"When did that ever stop you?"

She knew she shouldn't have said it, even if it were true. The sting of her mother's hand across her face stunned Riley. Corrine never lifted a finger to do anything. If she had called the maid in and instructed her to perform the slap for her, Riley would have been less surprised.

"Never again," She whispered.

"You have a smart mouth, Riley," Corrine said with a haughty look. "I should have done it years ago."

"Not the slap. I couldn't care less about that. You pack all the punch of an anemic gnat." Riley stepped toward her mother, feeling immense satisfaction when Corrine flinched.

"I'm your mother."

"It's a little late to play that card." Riley shook her head at Corrine's pathetic tactic. "I'm not going to hit you. Unless…"

"Unless what?" Corrine looked down her nose at Riley. It hadn't taken her long to regain her poise.

"Unless you ever touch Sean again."

Chapter Three

RILEY DIDN'T KNOW what Sean would say the next time they met.

She parked her car outside the Knights' headquarters. Gaige had called a tow truck after she and Sean left, texting her the details. Because it was an easy fix, the garage called early the next morning and she took a taxi to pick up her car.

There was an easy way out of this situation. She could stay away from Sean for the next few weeks. When they saw each other again, the awkwardness would dissipate quickly and they could pretend nothing had happened. Except, Riley didn't want to pretend. About the kiss, that is. Riley hoped Sean never mentioned her mother. Ever.

Giving her lip-gloss a quick check, Riley exited the car. She wasn't trying to be something she wasn't. A short skirt, tight top, and heels would have made her look as ridiculous as she would have felt. Different clothing wasn't going to make Sean look at her in a new way. That would take a change in attitude—from both of them.

How could Sean think of her as an exciting, interesting woman, if she didn't let him see that was who she was? Time to stop being tongue-tied. She was intelligent. Top of her class at business school. She kept up on current events and knew the Knights' playbook backward and forward. Riley could converse on almost any subject, and if he were willing to teach her, she would be an eager student when it came to sex. There was no reason for Sean to be bored—in or out of the bedroom.

She climbed into the stands, keeping out of sight so she could watch the end of practice. Harry Coleman didn't like distractions of any kind. She stayed in the shadows, waiting for Sean to do something. Anything.

As fate would have it, Riley was given a welcome and unexpected treat. Sean ran a slant route, his footwork fast and sure. The defensive end tried to keep up, but the rookie was no match for Sean's superior speed and experience.

Faking left, he dodged behind another member of the defense. A reverse screen. By the time the rookie figured out what was happening, Sean had caught the laser shot from Gaige, tucked the ball under his arm, and was halfway to the end zone.

Silently, Riley applauded. Sean was wonderful. One of the best in the game. However, it wasn't the play that made her heartbeat race. It was Sean's joy over a simple practice play. His laughter reached into the stands, wrapping itself around her like a warm hug. His smile was infectious. He didn't know she was there, yet it felt like he smiled just for her.

"You need to stop this, Riley."

Closing her eyes, Riley took a deep breath. Straightening her shoulders, she turned to her father.

"Stop watching the Knights? We both know that will never happen."

"Don't be coy. It doesn't suit you."

"Define coy," Riley said, tongue firmly in cheek.

"God, you are so much like your grandfather." One side of Gerald Preston's mouth curled into a sneer.

"Thank you."

"It wasn't meant as a compliment."

"I know. Yet that's how I choose to take it."

Gerald Preston was a handsome man. Tall, lean. His dark hair was still thick with only a touch of gray beginning to show. He kept himself fit. His personal trainer visited the house three times a week and he ran five miles every day. At fifty-three, he had the body of a much younger man.

Some people had commented on the resemblance between father and daughter. The same slender build. The blue eyes. The dark hair. Riley supposed it was true. When asked, she said she looked like her grandfather.

Riley felt a twinge of regret. It didn't happen often. Not anymore. There had been a time, just after her grandfather's death, when she wished for a closer relationship with her father. For twelve years, she had been blessed with a strong, loving male figure in her life. She felt the loss greatly.

Until then, she hadn't worried about the ice that dripped from her father's every word. She had Grandpa. However, without Douglas Preston's warm presence, Riley naturally looked to the man who had given her life. The man who had never shown an ounce of interest in her. She wasn't surprised to find out that hadn't changed. Disappointed, but not surprised.

"You hide up here in the stands, watching Sean McBride, thinking you're invisible. Trust me, *little girl*, he is the only one who doesn't know how you feel."

"I don't know what you mean."

Riley lifted her chin, trying to put on a brave face. Was her father right? Did everyone know? It was hard to know for certain. Her father didn't speak to her often, but when he did, it was never a pleasant experience. Where her grandfather had been full of laughter and good humor, her father was much more of a doom and gloom personality.

"That's a good poker face. Another of your grandfather's traits." Gerald casually picked a tiny piece of lint from his perfectly tailored suit. Flicking it away, his eyes met Riley's. The gesture wasn't random. Without words, he told her she was as insignificant as that piece of lint. And as easily taken care of.

If her father had spent any time getting to know her, he would have known Riley couldn't be intimidated that easily. Push her, she pushed back. That, too, was something she inherited from her grandfather.

"I have every right to be here." Riley refused to break eye contact. She felt a small thrill of accomplishment when he was the first to look away.

"You'll own the team someday." As always, Gerald had trouble saying the words. "It doesn't give you rights to the players."

"I repeat, I don't know what you mean."

"What is the appeal?" Gerald continued as though Riley hadn't spoken. "Sean McBride draws women like moths to a flame. I suppose he's attractive enough."

Riley snorted. *Attractive enough?* The man was a God!

"He's an outstanding athlete. An asset to the team. That is my only interest."

It sounded lame, even to her. Riley might not fool her father, but she wouldn't discuss her feelings about Sean. Not with him.

"Even your mother has commented on your unhealthy obsession."

That was interesting. Her mother and father rarely spoke. They led separate lives. It seemed unlikely they would break that precedent to discuss her.

The image of her mother touching Sean popped into Riley's head. Perhaps she wasn't the only Preston obsessed with the star wide receiver. The idea of Corrine making a move on Sean made Riley sick to her stomach. Would Sean turn her mother down? She was a beautiful woman. Sean was… Well, Sean was Sean. Riley wanted to believe he had some sexual line he wouldn't cross. A married woman? The owner's wife? If presented with the temptation, Riley had no idea which way Sean would leap.

For a brief moment, Riley considered mentioning how touchy-feely Corrine had been with Sean. Unfortunately, it would hurt Sean more than her mother. Gerald didn't care what his wife did, as long as she was discreet. Her parents had an open marriage, sleeping with other people whenever the impulse struck. The world saw them as a power couple. He was the powerful businessman, she the society hostess. They smiled for the cameras, looking happy and content.

She had no power on that front. So she kept her mouth shut. As far as she was concerned, her mother had never dipped her adulterous toe into the Knights' locker room. However, Riley knew the score. Corrine would walk away scot-free. Sean would be the one to pay.

"Is there a point to this conversation?" Riley wanted her father to leave. Practice was breaking up and she needed to speak with Sean. Without her father as a witness.

"Those men represent money." Gerald gestured toward the field. "You said it yourself. Sean McBride is an asset."

"So?"

"Here's a piece of advice they won't teach in any of your business classes. You can screw around with anyone you want." Gerald's cool eyes stayed on the field. "But never, ever, screw an asset. Especially one as valuable as Sean McBride."

Gerald didn't wait for Riley's response. She watched him head out of the exit. Her father's words didn't bother her. She took them in the spirit they were intended. Petty and cruel. This had been the longest conversation she could remember having with him in months. Had he asked about school or her health? Or anything a normal father would ask his daughter? No. Gerald Preston had no interest in her unless it was to leave the proverbial turd in her punch bowl.

"SHE'S UP THERE again."

Gaige didn't need to look at the stands. He knew who Sol meant.

"Riley loves this team."

"True," Sol nodded, stretching out his hamstring. "If push came to shove, which do you think she would choose? The team? Or Sean?"

"It's a moot point, so stop speculating. Now!"

"*Moot point*," Sol laughed. "Your fancy ass school roots are showing, QB."

"Says the man with a degree from Stanford." Gaige punched the linebacker in the arm. Hard. "They don't give those scholarships to dummies."

"Shh," Sol looked around in mock horror. "You'll ruin my reputation. My wife married me for my body, not my brains."

"What's the joke?" Sean asked, joining them on the sidelines. "After yesterday, I could use a chuckle."

"Did Mrs. Preston leave a mark on your baby-soft skin?" Sol's ham-like fist crashed into Sean's bicep. He wanted to hit Gaige back. However, his QB's arm was the team's bread and butter. That meant he had to take his revenge out on the unsuspecting running back.

"What the hell, Bellows?" Sean didn't rub his arm. That was the pussy thing to do. But, damn, it hurt.

"Watch the language."

"What? Where?" Sean looked around. He had told his teammates about Mrs. Preston. He had kept the kiss to himself. If it weren't for her mother, he would have spoken to Riley right away.He wanted to clear the air and this would be as good a time as any.

"Up in the stands."

"Sol!" Gaige warned.

"How long has she been up there?" Sean searched the seats. If Riley were there, he couldn't see her.

"You mean how often? Don't give me that look, Gaige. Some of the guys are starting to talk."

"Which ones?" Gaige would put a stop to that.

"It's innocent teasing," Sol assured Gaige. "For now. Sean needs to nip it in the bud before it escalates."

"I guess you're right."

"The guys are making cracks about Riley?" Sean felt his blood begin to simmer. "Why?"

"Because of you."

"Me?" Sean gave Gaige an amazed look. "She's like a little sister. Everybody knows that."

"Riley doesn't."

The kiss. Sean thought it had been a spur of the moment impulse. If he were to believe Gaige and Sol, there was much more to it.

"How long?"

"Now that you know there's a problem? Ask her." Sean nodded, getting up. "Don't mess with her, Sean. She's not as confident as she acts."

"Jesus, Gaige." Sean spiked his helmet. If he weren't worried about the Riley situation, he would have enjoyed Sol's yelp when it bounced off the back of his head. "Do you think I would take her to bed?"

"Sex is always the first thing that pops into your head. Why is that?" Not expecting an answer, Gaige continued. "That's right. Manwhore."

"Fuck you."

"Do you deny it?" Gaige challenged.

"No."

Sean had no problem with the label. He liked sex. A lot. And he liked variety. Tall. Short. Curvy. Thin. Give him a big, heaping helping of it all. What he didn't like was the implication he would touch Riley in anything but a brotherly fashion.

Gaige pushed to his feet. He was sympathetic to Sean's dilemma. However, he wanted him to understand what had to be done.

"Hope, Sean. It can keep the tiniest of flames flickering. Don't let Riley walk away thinking there's a chance you'll change your mind. Be brutal."

Agitated, Sean ran a hand through his hair.

"I've never broken anyone's heart before." When Sol snorted, Sean shot him a dirty look. "Not on purpose."

"A manwhore with a heart of gold." Sol stood beside Gaige, watching Sean leave the field. "Hey. Don't look so glum. You did good."

Gaige shrugged. He had been in the league for eleven years. Sometimes it was hard to remember what it was like to be Sean's age. Hell. Had he *ever* been twenty-five? His old man used to accuse him of being too serious.

Forget the fucking football, Larry Benson would yell out when he was sober enough to speak coherently. *It's a fucking pipe dream, stupid.* Then he would hurl an empty vodka bottle at Gaige's head. He became adept at dodging the projectiles. Practice for a life spent evading determined defensive ends.

It was ironic that a man who had grown up with that warped example would now be giving fatherly advice.

"Need to get home right away?"

"Nope." Sol slung a companionable arm over Gaige's shoulders. "The wife and kids are having dinner with her mother."

"How did you get out of that?" Sol's contentious relationship with his mother-in-law was the stuff of legend.

"Big game on Sunday. I need to study my playbook."

"Racine fell for that?"

"Hell, no," Sol laughed. "She knows all my tricks."

"So she let you get away with one?" Gaige and Sol grabbed their helmets. Without a second thought, Gaige picked up Sean's.

"Mmm. I love my wife."

"Me too." Racine Bellows was one of the good ones. A football wife who supported her husband and wasn't obsessed with pursuing her own fame on his coattails.

"My woman, Benson." Sol pounded his chest, caveman style.

"You have to admit, my taste is impeccable."

Sol laughed. "Yes, it is." He held the door for Gaige. "Beer at *The Extra Point*?"

The crowded locker room smelled like sweat and antiseptic. For Gaige, they were the most natural aromas in the world. Several of their teammates heard Sol's comment and before he knew it, half a dozen Knights were sharing long necks and laughs.

This was his family, Gaige thought, the noise around him welcome. Three thousand miles away from his abuse-filled childhood, he had found his place in the world. It wouldn't last forever, but for now, it was pretty damn perfect.

RILEY WAS STILL mulling over her father's words when the sound of approaching feet reached her. *Now who*, she wondered. Annoyed, she turned her head.

"Sean!" Riley smiled in delighted surprise.

He was still in his practice gear including full pads. His dark hair was damp and slightly matted from the helmet he must have left on the field. His face was flushed, sweat covering his brow. He looked like a warrior returning from battle. Fancifully, Riley pictured herself opening her arms in welcome. In her dreams, he would gather her close, happy to be home. Then—

"Riley!" She jumped when Sean snapped his fingers in front of her face. "Are you in there?"

"Sorry." Why was she daydreaming about Sean when he was right there? The real thing was so much better.

"You were a million miles away." Sean tilted his head to the side, his lips curving slightly. "I saw your dad up here. Did he upset you?"

"No." Riley didn't want to talk about her father. "I came to see you. I want to apologize about yesterday."

"I thought that might be why you were here." He shook his head. "There isn't any need. It was just a kiss. Let's forget it, okay?"

The kiss? Sean thought she wanted to apologize for kissing him?

"I'm not sorry I kissed you, Sean." Riley touched his arm. When he didn't move away, she felt emboldened. "I'm sorry my mother came on to you. It was embarrassing. Though I suppose you're used to that kind of thing. Women must throw themselves at you all the time."

Riley didn't see the irony of her words. To her love-hazed brain, her mother's actions were wrong. Her own were justifiable. She wasn't looking for a one-night conquest. Her feelings were deep. Genuine.

"Riley. There is something I need to say."

Sean stepped closer. It was the wrong move. Instead of seeing a man intent on letting her down gently, Riley saw what she wanted to see. She threw her arms around his waist, plastering her body to his. He smelled wonderful. His sweat clean and spicy.

"I love you, Sean."

"No, you don't." Kindly, Sean returned Riley's hug. "This is a crush."

"It's love," Riley said, her voice firm. "I've loved you for three years. I'll love you three years from now. I'll love you forever."

"Can we sit?"

Reluctantly, Riley stepped back. Sean flipped down two of the hard, plastic seats, then waited for her to join him.

"I know what you're going to say."

"Probably," Sean nodded. "You're the smartest person I know. You know what we're all thinking. Make me happy and humor me this one time."

Knowing he was teasing, Riley smiled. "Fine. But you won't change my mind."

"Why are you in love with me, Riley?"

Surprised, Riley blinked. Why? Why did anyone fall in love? There had to be a specific reason?

"I don't understand what you mean?"

"You don't know anything about me, Riley. Nothing important. God knows, I'm no expert. If you loved me, really loved me, you would know more than what is in my team bio."

"What makes you think I don't?"

"Fine." Sean gave her an indulgent smile. "Tell me something besides where I was born or how many siblings I have."

"You love the color blue."

"That's all you've got?"

Riley's eyes narrowed. She hated that condescending tone—especially when it came from Sean.

"Deep down, you wanted to be drafted by the Chicago Bears. Your dad is a big fan. Or was. He switched allegiances when you signed with the Knights. Your dream was to be a running back, like Walter Peyton. You had his poster on your closet door when you were growing up."

"Riley—"

"You had a dog named Grover. A mutt that followed you home from school when you were nine. Your mother allowed you to keep him and it almost killed you when he had to be put down your sophomore year of college."

"How do you know all of that?" Sean frowned. He knew he had never spoken of those things with Riley.

"I listen." Riley wanted to reach for his hand but restrained herself. "Three years, Sean. There were times when you didn't notice me. Practice. A party. After a few beers, you like to reminisce. I've learned a lot because I care. I love you."

"You have to stop saying that, Riley."

"Not saying it won't stop it from being true."

Her earnest expression was almost Sean's undoing. He wanted to gather her close and tell her it would be all right. Then he remembered Gaige's advice. He had to kill Riley's hope. It would be like crushing a butterfly emerging from its cocoon, but he knew in the long run, he would be doing her a favor.

"Do you know what I'm going to do tonight?"

"Have a beer with the guys. Pick up a woman. Have sex. Forget her name before you have your first cup of coffee the next morning?"

Jesus, she did know him. Sean's resolve stiffened. All the more reason to end this silly crush right now.

"Then I'll do it again. And again. And again."

"But—"

"I can see that mind of yours working." Sean sighed. "Forget it. You can't fix me because I'm not broken. I didn't have a horrible childhood. I wasn't abused or misused. I'm famous, rich, young, and healthy. There is an endless supply of willing women out there, Riley. One—sometimes two or three—for every day of my life. Why would I settle for the same meal day after day when my palate demands something wild and exotic?"

"I'm not asking you to change."

"Then what do you want, Riley?" Sean demanded. He knew what he wanted. This. Over. Now.

"You."

"Shit. And, no, I'm not going to apologize for swearing." Sean ran a distracted hand through his hair. "Open your ears. We are never going to happen."

"Why?"

"Too young. Too inexperienced. Too naive." Sean ticked each off on his fingers.

"Those things I can change." Riley reasoned. "Except the too young part. But with more experience, I won't seem as young. Or naive."

"You could fuck a hundred guys a hundred different ways, Riley. It wouldn't change the most important fact. I'm not attracted to you. I don't want you. Not now. Not ever."

Her mother's slap hadn't fazed her. However, Sean's words felt like a punch to the stomach. For a moment, Riley couldn't breathe. The pain was sharp. Intense. It was all she could do not to double over. Tears filled her eyes. Mortified, she turned away. She never let anyone see her cry. Not her parents. Not her friends. She refused to let Sean be the exception.

Without a word or a backward glance, Riley ran.

Sean almost called out to her. It killed him to know he caused her pain. He liked Riley. Truly liked her. However, seeing the unadulterated hero-worship shining from her eyes had made him uncomfortable. No one could live with those kinds of expectations. One day he was bound to disappoint her. Better now while she was young.

Riley believed her heart was broken. Sean knew better. It was dinged. She had been crushed by her crush. In a few days, a week at the most, she would laugh at her foolishness. Their first meeting would be a little awkward. Then things could go back to normal. Friends. Brother and sister. That was how they would go forward. They would put today in the rearview mirror.

Satisfied that he had done a good thing, Sean headed to the locker room, blissfully unaware of the wheels he had set in motion.

Chapter Four

IT WAS TWO weeks later and Riley still wasn't laughing. Her heart that Sean so blithely believed was only dinged, was a constant ache in her chest. She couldn't sleep or eat. The only thing that got her up and out of her bedroom was school. That one constant gave her a purpose. A goal.

Winter break was fast approaching. A month without classes. Riley had no idea what she would do with the time.

Her world had been turned on its side. After three years, in a few short minutes, Sean had destroyed her dreams. It didn't matter how unrealistic they had been. Or that Sean had never given her an ounce of encouragement. There had always been a spark of hope. Now there was none.

"Your mother insists that you stop moping around your room," Veronica Trumbo informed Riley."It is unacceptable for you to miss family dinners when your parents are entertaining guests."

Her mother's personal assistant often delivered messages. Corrine didn't care what bothered her daughter. She cared how it looked to the outside world.

"We don't have family dinners. We have business meetings."

"Which you are expected to attend. Your mother insists."

Riley stared out the window. She was bundled in her favorite blanket, sitting in the cozy little nook window. The trees that filled her view never changed. Tall pines, green all year round. Riley loved those trees. Their scent filled her room on warm summer nights. Simply looking at them could soothe her like nothing else. The way she felt at the moment, they might as well have been a cement wall.

"My mother can stick it up her—"

"Miss Preston!"

"Go away." Riley couldn't stir up enough interest to argue. "Let me know the next time they need to put me on display. I'll be there."

"Your lack of familial loyalty is appalling," Veronica sniffed.

"Yeah. I'm a fucking ingrate."

"That kind of language is unacceptable, young lady. It's offensive and vulgar."

"Then cover your ears, or leave the room. I'm about to let loose with words that will peel the paint off the walls."

She turned her head, her eyes boring into Veronica. The woman didn't deserve Riley's ire. She was doing her job. It was a case of wrong place, wrong time. Riley needed to vent, and Veronica was the only one handy.

"Still here?"

"Miss Preston. You are well educated. Cursing shows a woeful lack of imagination and creativity."

"I disagree. Listen to how imaginative and creative I can be."

She let loose a string of expletives so colorful Veronica almost fainted from the shock. For the first time in weeks, Riley felt like smiling. *Thank you, Grandpa.* He had never seen anything wrong with teaching a young girl how to express herself. He had warned her to use the words judiciously. Until today, Riley seldom swore. However, now that she had started, it felt better than she could have imagined.

"Your mother will hear about this."

Red-faced, Veronica hurried from the room.

"Then she can send you back with her disapproval," Riley yelled. Then she muttered, "Bitch."

35

"Impressive."

Riley's eyes widened. *Gaige*. Where had he come from? Knowing he must have heard every word she spewed at Veronica, Riley felt her cheeks heat.

"I'm not going to apologize," she said, her chin jutting out.

"Why would I ask you to?"

The room was meant for a small girl. Her grandfather had it decorated with her favorite colors. Purple and pink. Riley's tastes had changed considerably in twelve years, but she hadn't been able to change a single thing. The frilly canopy bed, the Hello Kitty wallpaper.

Riley hadn't thought about it until now. Gaige made the room seem twice as small and three times as childish. Sean's words rang in her head. Immature. Between her childish outburst and the pink elephant floor lamp, she realized it would be hard to argue the point if he suddenly walked in.

Having Gaige witness it was almost as bad.

"Why are you here?"

"It's been a while since we've seen you around the complex."

"Oh, God." Riley covered her face with the blanket. "He told you."

"Sean is worried about you, Riley. We all are."

"All? He told *all* of you? The whole team?"

"Mind if I join you?"

Riley slid to the side. The window seat wasn't very big. Somehow Gaige wedged himself into the limited space.

"Can you breathe under there?"

With a sigh, Riley lowered the blanket.

"What?" she huffed, pushing back her dark hair. She hadn't combed it today. Riley wondered what she looked like, then decided she didn't care. Gaige hadn't been invited. He would have to take her as he found her. Rat's nest hair and all.

Gaige smiled, his green eyes warm with concern.

"In Sean's defense, the team already knew how you felt."

"Are you trying to make me feel worse?"

Gaige grabbed the blanket before she could disappear again.

"Riley…"

"Not you too." She shook her head. "It isn't a crush, Gaige. Not that it matters. I'm unfuckable."

"Jesus, Riley. What the hell did Sean say to you?"

"He wants heat—spice." Riley curled into a tight ball. "I'm boring and inexperienced. Like a cold bowl of pablum. To quote the man himself, he wouldn't screw me if I were the last woman on earth."

"Idiot," Gaige grumbled. "Come here."

It took some doing, but Gaige untangled her limbs then pulled her into his arms. With a weary sigh, Riley slowly relaxed. The last person to hold her like this had been her grandfather. Feeling close to tears, she realized how much she had missed being held and comforted.

"You aren't un— Gaige hesitated. "You know what I want to say."

"Yes." Riley nodded. "It wasn't the words, Gaige. It was the person who said them. He wanted to hurt me and I don't know why."

"It's my fault."

Riley shook her head. "I know you think you have control over every member of the team, but Sean is a big boy."

"I told him to speak to you."

"What?" Riley's body tensed. "Why?"

"To spare you this." Gaige squeezed her hand. "I messed up."

Jumping to her feet, Riley rounded on Gaige. "It wasn't up to you. My heart. My heartbreak. God!" She closed her eyes, fists clenched. "What is wrong with me?"

"Nothing."

"Really?" Riley met his gaze. The sadness in her eyes tore at Gaige's heart. "My parents have no use for me unless they are trying to present themselves as the perfect family. Sean thinks I'm a boring virgin. Not so far off, it would seem."

"Riley."

"And you." Riley swallowed the lump in her throat. "My hero. That's how I've always thought of you. It hurts to find out you have no confidence in me."

"Why do you say that?" Gaige frowned.

"You don't think I'm capable of handling my feelings for Sean."

"I made a mistake. I'm sorry."

"So am I." Riley sat down, wrapping the blanket around herself—shutting out the world. Shutting out Gaige. "Leave."

Gaige slowly walked to the door. At the last moment, he turned back. "You shouldn't be alone."

"Don't worry about me." Hugging her knees, Riley looked out at the trees. "I'm used to it."

ENTERING THE BAR, Riley looked around.

It was two in the afternoon—the week between Christmas and the new year. *The Extra Point* wasn't exactly hopping with activity. A man and woman sat at the bar, nursing beers, and lamenting the end of another year. On the jukebox, Nat King Cole sang of a Mona Lisa smile. In the corner, a lone figure knocked balls around a pool table.

Hanging her umbrella on a row of pegs by the door, Riley crossed the room. She felt nervous. Uncertain. For the first time, she wasn't sure of what her reception would be. When he looked up and smiled, Riley smiled back. Her nerves melted.

"Want to play a game? Gaige held out his pool cue.

"Sure." Riley removed her jacket. Waiting while he took out the rack, she chalked the end of the stick. "Straight eight ball?"

Gaige nodded. "You break."

Riley moved to the end of the table and took aim. "I'm sorry." She struck the white ball with at clean, hard stroke.

"You were right to be mad," Gaige said, watching two solid balls fall into opposite pockets. "I had no right to interfere."

"You meant well. You always do. After I had time to cool down, I realized you were right."

Gaige didn't answer. He waited while Riley ran the table. There was a beauty to her movements. Sure and easy. An athlete of sorts—though she would have scoffed at the idea.

"Why do I bother?" He asked when the eight ball disappeared into the side pocket.

"If you didn't want me to beat you, you never should have taught me the game."

Riley had been thirteen and still reeling from her grandfather's death. Gaige hadn't thought anything of it at the time. He and the rest of the Knights were attending a party at the Preston mansion. A few of them were playing pool in the game room when he noticed the gangly girl with big blue eyes watching. She looked so lonely. Showing her the basics of the game had been a careless gesture of kindness. The friendship that had grown between them had been a surprise. And a blessing—for both of them.

"You took to it like a duck to water."

Riley laughed. "I practiced every day."

"I figured."

Gaige held out a chair. A mug of hot chocolate was set in front of her.

"Thanks, Wayne," Riley said.

The owner of the bar winked before clearing off some empty glasses from a nearby table. Gaige sipped his beer, waiting.

"I feel like I've been kicked out of a three-year haze. A big fat, Sean McBride haze."

"And?"

"I'm bruised, but healing." And still very much in love. However, she didn't need to tell Gaige that. He already knew. Somehow, he always knew. "The truth is, I feel like a fool."

"There's nothing wrong with loving someone, Riley," Gaige said. "I know it hurts, but having an open heart is a good thing. You're one of the lucky ones. There are people who are incapable of loving anyone but themselves."

Riley frowned at Gaige's words. She was so used to him having all the answers, it was easy to forget that Gaige Benson was as human as the rest of the world.

"We all come to you with our problems." Riley laid her hand over his. "Who do you talk to?"

"Me?" Gaige laughed. He tried, but it didn't quite reach his eyes. "Haven't you heard? I have it all."

Riley would have pushed the issue, but Gaige changed the subject. Because she cared, she let him.

"School starts in a few weeks."

"Not for me."

"You're dropping out?" Outrage vibrated in his voice. "You can't."

"I'm not dropping out," she reassured him. "I'm leaving."

"Seattle? Where are you going?"

"East. I've never told anyone this." Riley looked a little sheepish. "I was accepted to Harvard. I don't have to tell you why I chose the University of Washington instead."

"Oh, honey."

"It doesn't matter." Riley shrugged. "I'm going to stay with friends in Boston. Amazingly, Harvard still wants me."

"Of course, they do." Gaige smiled. "Two years. I'll miss you."

"I'll miss you, too."

Riley sighed. She looked at Gaige, wondering why she couldn't have fallen in love with him. He was gorgeous. Tall. Powerful. Women swooned over his blond hair and green eyes. He was the real deal. And she *did* love him. As a friend.

"What's with the mysterious smile?"

"What would I have done if you had never taught me to play pool?"

"You're strong," Gaige said. "You would have been fine. I, on the other hand, would have missed out on watching a precocious girl grow into an amazing woman."

The look that passed between them said it all. Respect. Affection. Love. Gaige would always be there for her—no matter where she was in the world.

"I have to go." Reaching for her jacket, her lips curved, her smile tinged with sadness and irony. "I'll never be old enough for him, will I?"

"Sean had it wrong, Riley. You aren't too young for him. He's too young for you."

"What?"

"He's a little boy," Gaige explained. "Everything is a game. Football. Women. Life. He's Peter Pan."

"He looks all grown up." *Boy. Did he ever*, Riley thought, picturing Sean's beautiful body.

"On the outside. Until his brain catches up, he won't be ready for you, Riley." Gaige's eyes were sympathetic. "It might never happen."

"And I can't wait around hoping it will."

Gaige helped her on with her jacket.

"Keep in touch."

Riley returned his hug. She felt safe with Gaige's arms around her and for a moment, she was tempted to throw away her plans. Seattle was her home. The Knights were in the playoffs. How could she leave?

"Hey, Riley."

Because all it took was the sound of Sean's voice and she wanted to fall to her knees. *Love me*, she would beg. *Why won't you love me?*

"Are you okay?" Gaige whispered.

Riley nodded. She straightened her shoulders, shored up her resolve, and turned.

"How was your Christmas, Sean?"

"Terrific. I flew my parents in."

"That's nice," she said as though nothing between them had changed.

Riley could see the relief in his eyes. There would be no recriminations. No embarrassing scene. Sean was off the hook. More than he knew.

"Are you leaving?" he asked when she picked up her purse.

"I am." All the way across the country. Riley wondered what his reaction would be to that. Deciding she didn't need any more heartache, she kept it to herself.

"I'll see you around," he called out. Sean, being Sean, was already checking out the cute blond at the bar.

"Goodbye, Sean."

It was time to leave the old Riley behind. Not looking back, Riley opened the bar's front door and stepped into the Seattle mist one last time.

Chapter Five

FIVE YEARS LATER

RILEY PARKED TOWARD the back of the Knights' parking lot. She gave herself a moment to look around.

There were a few cosmetic changes. Fresh paint. The façade over the entrance showed the team's new logo. The updated Knight in blue and gold was more fierce—less cartoony than before.

For some reason, the change had been contentious among the shareholders. Something about upholding tradition. Yada, yada, yada. Six months ago, her opinion wouldn't have mattered. However, on her twenty-fifth birthday, Riley inherited another block of shares. Enough to make her an official voting member of the board.

Like any responsible adult, she weighed the issue carefully. Examined the facts. Perused the new logo. Then sent her vote of approval. The email from her father's assistant arrived an hour later accusing her of voting, not for the change, but against him.

It wasn't true. She thought the new logo was better. Modern. Riley knew without hesitation that her grandfather would have approved. She made all of her decisions concerning the team by first weighing how she thought Douglas Preston would have voted. In her mind, it was still his team. She wouldn't take over the team for another five years. Until that day, she considered herself an extension of him.

Thwarting her father had never been her goal. It simply turned out to be a nice bonus.

Riley opened her car door. It was late November and surprisingly warm by Seattle standards. The heels of her boots clicked as she walked to the building. The logo wasn't the only thing that had changed. Riley was different. Inside and out.

Anyone looking at her would see a sophisticated young woman. Which was exactly what she wanted. Riley had worked hard to polish off her rough edges. Gone were the ubiquitous blue jeans, sneakers, and Knights jersey. She was a successful businesswoman and it was important for her wardrobe to reflect it.

She had started from the bottom and worked up. Heels. *High* heels. It may have seemed like a small thing, but until she graduated from Harvard, Riley had never worn them. Flats were more practical for running around campus.

Starting with a pair of four-inch pumps had been a trifle ambitious, but that was Riley. She tackled every challenge with stubborn determination. From the world economics class that seemed like Greek her first week—she ended up getting an A—to traversing the ins and outs of the dating world. When Riley put her mind to something, she succeeded.

Riley's first few dates hadn't worked out well. She had been stiff and uncomfortable. However, she kept at it until she didn't have to think about smiling or laughing—or talking. Some of the men she met had intrigued her enough to move on to a second date. And a third. A few had gained boyfriend status. A couple had become lovers. Nothing serious, but nice. One was still a good friend.

All in all, her love life was… nice. Successful, if not spectacular.

The high heels were another matter. That endeavor quickly morphed from wobbly experiment to what she assumed would be a lifelong love affair. Soon, she was walking around like she had been born wearing stilettos. The added height gave her confidence. Most days it was like gilding the lily. The one thing the new Riley Preston didn't lack was a belief in herself and her abilities.

However, today she felt a bit shaky. She took a deep breath. This, the Knights' headquarters, was the site of her greatest defeat.

Sean McBride.

Riley didn't think of him very often. Not anymore. He was a part of her past. An important part. Her three-year obsession. Four, if she were honest. It took her a year to gain perspective. *Out of sight, out of mind.* It hadn't seemed possible when she was twenty with a bleeding heart, but eventually, it became the truth—not just a well-worn adage.

Confronting her demons was the final step to putting the past behind her for good. Today was the first step in that journey. Visiting the Knights' facility late on a Monday afternoon—when she was certain Sean wasn't likely to be around—wasn't cowardly, she assured herself. It was her way of easing into her old life. The fewer bumps, the better.

The receptionist looked up from behind her desk. The sleek blonde's automatic smile didn't mask the woman's none-too-subtle once over. Riley recognized the look. *Who is this and is she worth my precious time?* Making a mental note to keep her eye on—Riley read the woman's name tag—Carrie, she plastered on her own fake smile.

"May I help you?" Carrie asked.

"I need a pass." Riley reached into her purse for her ID.

"Are you expected?"

"No." *That was putting it mildly.* Her father would not be happy to see her.

"Then I can't help you." This time, Carrie's smile was genuine.

"You could if you wanted to." Riley slapped her driver's license onto the counter. "The name is Riley Preston." When the woman's eyes widened, Riley nodded. "Yes, that Preston."

"I'm sorry, Ms. Preston." Opening the top desk drawer, Carrie fumbled with several clip-on badges. "I only have guest passes. I'm sure you can go on through without one."

Riley took the badge. "I'd rather not have to explain myself every time I meet a new face. And Carrie?"

"Yes?"

"From now on, I'll be coming in every day. I want to see you treat everyone who walks through those doors with the utmost courtesy. Understood?" Riley didn't add, *your job depends on it*, but from the look on Carrie's face, it wasn't necessary.

"Of course, Ms. Preston."

Walking to the elevator, Riley wondered how long it would take for news of her arrival to travel through the building. She punched the button for the fifth floor. As the doors closed, she spied Carrie on the phone, speaking animatedly. When she reached her floor, another woman, brunette instead of blond, was there to greet her. Other than the color of her hair, the women could have been twins.

It seemed large breasts were the overriding hiring criteria at Knights' headquarters these days. Under a double-D need not apply. Riley didn't bother to look down. With her chest, it was a good thing she was born a Preston. With her meager endowments, she wouldn't have been allowed into the building.

"Ms. Preston. My name is Sapphire. I'm one of your father's personal assistants."

Riley shook Sapphire's proffered hand.

One of them? Unable to help herself, Riley asked, "How many does he need?"

"There seems to be a new one every week."

Laughing with delight, Riley ran to the tall blond man, throwing herself into his waiting arms.

"Gaige." Riley savored the moment. The feel of his strong arms holding her close was a treat she had missed.

"It's been a crappy day, Riley. Until now." Gaige swung her around. "Why didn't you tell me you were coming when we spoke on Sunday?"

After the game, a phone call had become a ritual. Win or lose, Gaige always called. Unfortunately, the last couple of years there had been more reason to commiserate than celebrate.

"I was leaving the window open in case I changed my mind." *Or chickened out.* "I didn't expect to see any players at this time of the day."

"Just me," he reassured her. "I had a meeting with some of the board members."

"Pardon me, Mr. Benson." Riley saw the predatory look in Sapphire's eyes. The woman liked what she saw. From the expression on Gaige's face, it was obvious he didn't return her interest. "Need I remind you. Anything discussed in the corporate offices is not for dissemination."

"Why don't you scurry off to your boss and tell him I'll bring Riley along in few minutes."

"But—"

"Please?"

One sweetly phrased word, accompanied by his famous killer smile, was all it took. Sapphire's shoulders straightened, her chest jutting out to terrifying proportions.

"If you need anything, I'll be at my desk until six o'clock," she purred.

"How does she keep her balance?" Riley asked when Sapphire was out of earshot.

"You're asking the wrong person," Gaige shuddered.

"She's pretty—and interested." Riley sent him a teasing smile. "You haven't been tempted to take a bounce on her bazoombas?"

"And risk drowning if those implants popped? Credit me with more self-preservation than that."

Taking her arm, Gaige guided Riley to an empty sitting area. It wasn't very private, but it was comfortable and at this time of day, they weren't likely to be disturbed.

"There." Always the gentleman, Gaige seated her before taking the chair to her left. "Tell me why you changed your plans. I didn't expect to see you until April."

At least once a year Gaige visited her in Boston. The first time had come only a few months after she had left Seattle. She was homesick— her determination to make a fresh start crumbling. Gaige propped up her courage. Not by reminding her of all the reasons she had to stay away. Instead, he pointed out the many, many advantages to keeping on her new, healthier course.

Over time, his visits became less of a lifeline and more the simple enjoyment of getting together because they enjoyed each other's company. Riley wasn't sure when the change had occurred. At some point she was no longer the lonely girl Gaige had befriended; they were equals. Peers. Friends.

"I wanted to lend my support to your plan. I get the impression your meeting didn't go well?"

"Your father's vision for this team is myopic. We haven't had a winning season in three years. That isn't going to change unless he thinks outside the box."

Riley knew what Gaige had in mind and she was one hundred percent on board. She hated the idea of him retiring after next season. The Knights without Gaige Benson at the helm? It was a sad thought. However, she respected his need to retire on his own terms. He was still one of the best in the game. In her eyes, *the* best. He would be thirty-eight next year. Time to hang up his cleats.

Gaige had been playing football for over twenty years. He had every accolade the game could provide. There was only one thing he was missing. A ring. *The* ring. A Super Bowl victory. Whatever it took, he was determined to go out a winner

"The bye week is in early December." It was a statement, not a question.

Riley kept up with the team. The Knights would belong to her one day. It made sense to be on top of what was going on. Besides, she still loved the game. She had shed a lot of things from her past—that wasn't one of them.

"Week after next," Gaige nodded. "I had planned on heading to Oklahoma. Now, I'm not sure there is any point. I don't want to get Logan's hopes up if there's a chance I can't follow through. Life keeps knocking him down. If I can't give him a hand up, I'd rather not go."

"Don't change your plans."

"I spent an hour trying to bore through your father's thick skull. He gave me a flat out no, Riley."

Riley hadn't seen or spoken to her father in five years. All communication came through letters, emails, and texts—sent by a third party. A gift card at Christmas, a generic acknowledgment of her birthday. Not that she had been any better. Their relationship would never be close. Or warm. Or loving. Riley had come to terms with that while her grandfather was still alive.

Having a place to call home—with parents she could count on—would have been nice. However, that was not the case. Riley slowly smiled. It was unfortunate. But it made what she was about to do much easier.

"Don't change your plans."

"Riley," Gaige said warily. "I don't like that smile."

"Good." Her cool eyes met his. "My father has had things his own way for too long. That's about to change, Gaige. Starting now."

"YOU'LL HAVE TO wait until he's off the phone."

Riley wasn't in the mood. Sapphire blocked the door to Gerald Preston's office, her arms splayed against the wooden surface. *Hello, drama queen.*

She gave the woman points for loyalty. Either her father handed out an amazingly generous Christmas bonus or Sapphire imagined herself as the next Mrs. Preston. She wouldn't be the first to make that mistake. Short of death, nothing was breaking up her parents. It had been a match made in convenience heaven and continued to suit them perfectly.

"He did send you to meet me at the elevator."

"That was almost an hour ago. You kept him waiting."

Riley sighed. This wasn't one-upmanship, this was petty and juvenile. Taunts from the grade school bully. Her gaze pinned Sapphire to the door. Riley hadn't suffered bullies when she was ten. She wouldn't start now.

"Move."

"No." Sapphire's voice cracked, but she didn't budge.

"Do you realize how ridiculous you look?" It wouldn't hurt to try reason. "What if someone important walks in? Stories like this travel like wildfire. Do you want to be the lead story on TMZ?"

From the way Sapphire perked up, it appeared she would be fine with that. *I'm ready for my close-up, Mr. DeMille.*

"Have it your own way," Riley said with an angelic smile. "Dad!" When she wanted, Riley could bellow with the best of them. "Get out here before I give your assistant the black eye to end all black eyes."

Sapphire's bravado lasted less than ten seconds. When her body started to shake and tears filled her eyes, Riley took pity on her.

"Move," she told the woman. "He's not coming out to save you."

"He isn't, is he?" Sapphire wiped at the tears gathering in her eyes. Letting Riley pass, she whispered to herself, "The bastard."

Another woman disappointed by Gerald Preston, Riley thought. It was a long and varied list. They could start a club. A sad, pathetic club. *No thanks.* With a shake of her head, she entered the office.

"Did you enjoy that?" Riley asked the man behind the desk.

"If you choose to make a scene, that is up to you. It has nothing to do with me."

Her father didn't bother to look up from the paper he was reading. One more power play designed to make her feel small and insignificant. Riley knew the drill. She was supposed to stammer and fuss until she was such a bundle of nerves he could sweep her out the door with little effort. *Fat chance.* Gerald Preston had a lot to learn about his daughter.

Riley walked to the chair opposite her father's desk, took a seat, and waited. She had all day. Until he properly acknowledged her, she wasn't saying another word.

To pass the time, she looked around the office.

It had belonged to her grandfather at one time. Almost every day after school, Riley would join him here. She would do her homework on the desk he had made especially for her. It sat near the wall of windows and provided her a view of the small park to the south. He would go over team business while she did her homework.

Her desk was long gone—as were every other physical trace of Douglas Preston. However, the memories were strong and comforting. No amount of redecorating could remove those.

"Riley."

Score one for her. Proverbially, her father blinked first.

"Father."

Again, Riley waited. She enjoyed his surprise when he took in her appearance. Gerald would see the sleek, dark hair, the expensive dove gray leather jacket, and tailored wool pants. Her makeup was subtle, emphasizing her large, blue eyes.

What he didn't see—what he refused to see—was a strong, intelligent professional. Gone was the rag-tag college student who had haunted the corners of the stadium. She looked like what she was. A businesswoman to be reckoned with.

"That was quite an entrance." Gerald removed his reading glasses. "I had hoped your time away would have matured you. Apparently, I hoped in vain."

Riley smiled. Her father wanted to put her on the defensive? He was about to find out how much she had changed.

"Logan Price."

Her father raised an eyebrow. "What about him?"

"The Knights are going to issue him an official invitation to next year's training camp."

"Ah." Gerald sat back in his chair. The smile on his face condescendingly familiar. "I didn't realize Benson was such a whiney little girl. Did he cry on your shoulder?"

"Issue the invitation," Riley said calmly.

"No," Gerald responded. "You have more shares, Riley. Not more power."

Riley smiled. Her father didn't realize it, but he was setting this up perfectly.

"And that's what this is about, isn't it? Power. The team brings non-roster invitees into camp all the time. Normally you wouldn't blink an eye."

"True," Gerald drew out the word.

"You get pleasure from slapping people down. When it's someone you dislike, you revel in it."

"I admit, there is a certain satisfaction in taking Gaige Benson down a peg or two." Gerald sneered. "The man has an overinflated opinion of himself. He's an aging quarterback on a mediocre team."

"He's a quarterback at the top of his game who has no protection on his offensive line and no running game. That's on management, not him."

"Logan Price won't fix that." Riley could tell she'd hit a nerve.

"Draft better. That will help plug the holes on the line. Gaige believes Logan Price is worth a look. So do I."

"Why? You think the knee he blew out a few years ago is magically better? He tried to come back. It didn't work."

"If it doesn't work out, so what?" Riley knew her father wasn't going to budge. He rarely changed his mind because no one had the power to make him. Until now.

"The board could overturn your decision."

"They could," Gerald conceded. "But they won't. I have their full support. You would only embarrass yourself if you called for a vote."

"One of us will be embarrassed," Riley said smoothly. "It won't be me."

For the first time, Riley had Gerald's full attention. His blue eyes met hers. The color was one of the few things they had in common. That and his dark hair. She had her mother's build. She had inherited her grandfather's temperament and business savvy. Watching her father's eyes narrow with growing concern, she realized the color of their eyes really was the only thing they shared.

"I don't believe you."

"You don't have to." Riley crossed her legs. The tension in the room grew—and it all came from him. "Not that you noticed, but I graduated from college three years ago. Did you once stop to wonder what I've been doing all this time?"

"No."

Give the man points for honesty. Riley shook her head. In the face of his power crumbling around him, Gerald refused to cower. Good for him. He could stand tall as his ship sank. Right now, the water was waist high and rising fast.

"Since you asked so nicely, I'll tell you."

"Sarcasm?" Gerald scoffed. "Didn't they teach you better than that at Harvard?"

"I started my own business." Riley ignored her father's taunt. "A consulting firm. In my spare time, I mentor young women who want to be entrepreneurs."

"Fascinating." It was obvious Gerald wasn't impressed.

"Between consulting and mentoring, I'm working with over half of the board members."

"You don't say." Gerald shifted in his seat.

Feeling the heat? Riley wondered. "It's called networking. I'm sure you're familiar with the term."

"Mmm."

"Getting their votes would have been simple. All it would have taken was a gentle reminder that one day, in the not so distant future, I'll be running the team. However, that would have been the easy way out."

"God forbid you sink to that."

"Sarcasm? Tsk, tsk." Riley watched the color rise on her father's face. "I want allies, not lackeys."

The implication hung between them. Her father hired yes-men. His opinion was all that counted.

"I've earned their respect and loyalty with hard work."

"Money is everyone's bottom line, Riley."

She shrugged. "I've made them a lot of that, too."

"In other words, I'm fucked."

"That's one way of looking at it." Her father didn't use that kind of language often. She had broken through the final wall of resistance. "You have two choices. Fight me. Or work with me."

"Meaning?"

"Stay on as president of the Knights. No one has to know about this little power play. I don't want to run the Knights. Not yet."

"No?" Gerald's laugh held little humor. "Funny; that isn't how it feels."

"There's a reason Grandpa chose thirty instead of giving me the team when I graduated from college. He knew it would become my obsession—to the exclusion of everything else." Riley's expression softened. "I've had the chance to build a life away from here. I'm ready to bring football back into my life—gradually. There is still a lot I plan to do before I take over the team full time."

Maybe marriage. A child. She didn't share that with her father. Or mention the man whose face popped into her head when she thought of who would share those things with her. No! Absolutely not. Sean McBride had no part in her future except as a football player.

Riley was so shaken by her wayward thoughts, she missed part of what her father was saying.

"It's a game." Gerald slammed his hand onto his desk, inadvertently regaining her full attention. "He never understood that."

"You never understood." Riley wasn't sure he ever would, but she would try one last time. "After years of working for no other reason than to make money, Grandpa finally found his passion. His job never brought him joy. The Knights did."

"Isn't that sweet." Gerald stood, turning his back to her. "I could have ruined this team."

"You've tried." Riley resented her father's passive-aggressive attitude toward her and the Knights. "You've cut salaries. Used your influence to make poor draft picks. If it weren't for Gaige and—" she choked back Sean's name. She wasn't giving her father that weapon to toss at her. "Your power has never been limitless."

"No. My father made certain of that."

"What's it going to be?"

They circled back to where they started. A familiar journey with no change in the destination. She would never understand her father and he would never try to understand her.

Stalemate.

"I stay in charge?"

"With increased input from me." Riley couldn't see her father's face, but she imagined a lot of eye rolling. "Not directly. I'll take my place on the board. Unless you decide to go rogue, this is the last time we will deal one on one."

"Go rogue." Gerald clasped his hands behind his back. "An interesting turn of phrase. Isn't that what you've done?"

"No. I'm moving toward a foregone conclusion."

Riley knew this was a bitter pill for her father to swallow. It meant so many things. He was growing older. She was coming into her own. Some parents wanted that for their children. Not Gerald Preston. Not if it was at his expense.

"I won't fight you." He was pragmatic enough to understand what was happening. He'd lost. Battle and war.

"You needn't be so glum. We're going to make the Knights contenders. In five years, when you turn over the reins, this team will be a winner and you'll get the credit."

Slowly, Gerald turned, his face void of emotion. As was his voice.

"I don't want this team to win."

Riley could have rubbed salt in the wound. Inside, she was doing a happy dance to end all happy dances. However, she was content with leaving her father with one parting shot.

"You can't stop them. Not anymore."

SEAN WATCHED HIS date swivel her hips in rhythm to the music blasting from the club's hidden speakers. They were nice hips. Above average—like the rest of her. She knew how to dance. If he recalled, the Rumba was her specialty. Or was it Zumba? Hell, it was so loud in here he had stopped making any effort to hear her an hour ago.

It was official. He was getting old. When a willing woman in a skin-tight miniskirt couldn't hold his attention, it was either the first sign of the apocalypse, or Sean McBride's wild days were waning. Fast.

Sean waited for the feeling of panic. Or sadness. Or, at the very least, a few moments of bittersweet regret. When none of those emotions came, he felt like laughing. Well, shit. Was this what becoming a mature adult felt like? It wasn't as bad as he had always feared.

"Want another beer?"

The barmaid's lips brushed his ear. Even with the pounding music, it was closer than necessary. Sean ignored the obvious come on. He didn't pick up women when he was already with one—not anymore.

"I'm good, thanks."

With a shrug, she returned Sean's smile. She cleared off the empties from a nearby table, sent him one last hopeful look, then moved on.

"You're slipping, son." Pete Jacobs took a long pull from the bottle in his hand. "Not that long ago, you would have left with the waitress—*and* Simone."

Pete kicked field goals and extra points for the Knights. Some thought that meant he wasn't a real athlete. Sean and the rest of his teammates didn't care what anyone said. Pete never missed. Never. That made him all the athlete they needed.

"I'm thirty."

Pete snorted, spitting his beer down his chin.

"What does that mean? Look at the old man. Age isn't slowing him down."

Gaige Benson was thirty-eight. He had a woman in front of him, one in back, and a couple of spares ready to take their turn. Their QB had the moves, Sean admitted. On and off the field.

"I've been full out manwhoring for fifteen years," Sean said with a self-deprecating smile. "Gaige has paced himself. He could go for another ten years—my motor could blow at any minute."

Pete blinked, looked at his beer, then blinked again. "Just to be clear, we *are* talking about sex, right?"

"Right," Sean clinked his bottle against Pete's.

"Good. This country boy can't always keep up with your big city metaphors."

This time, it was Sean whose beer spewed across the table. Pete loved to play up his Georgia roots. And play down his master's degree in English literature. One moment he was all slow-talk and cornpone, the next he was spouting Shakespearean soliloquies.

Was there another creature as contradictory as a football player? Sean wondered. Even Gaige. Off the field, he was the most stable man you could meet—ninety-nine percent of the time. Then, seemingly without warning, a mood would hit him. Tonight was one of those times.

Sean had no idea what drove Gaige on nights like this. They had been friends and teammates for almost eight years. The QB lent a sympathetic ear to anyone who needed it. Yet Sean couldn't recall him unburdening himself. Not about anything serious.

With Sean, what you saw was what you got. Gaige appeared to be the same way. However, his closest friends knew the truth. There were hidden depths behind those affable green eyes. Dark. Dangerous. One saw it on the field. During a game, Gaige was one scary motherfucker.

"I like Casanova Gaige." Pete chuckled when the women decided to link arms, circling Gaige with their writhing bodies. "It beats Biker Gang Gaige any day."

"One time," Sean said. "And he wasn't part of the gang. Called one of them blubber butt."

Who knew leather-clad men with scary tattoos were so sensitive? The fight hadn't lasted long. The gang were Knights' fans. They didn't want Gaige busting up his hand. Each man was allowed one punch. To his satisfaction, Gaige did a lot more damage than blubber butt.

"Biker Gang Gaige has a nice ring to it. I'm sticking with it."

"Fine. Just don't let him hear you."

Gaige went off the rails once or twice a year—that Sean knew of. The incidents lasted one night. The rule was, no one spoke of it. Ever.

"Hey, baby." Simone slithered onto Sean's lap. She was a sweet woman with the unfortunate tendency to wear too much perfume and call him baby. He put up with it because she gave killer head. "Want to go back to my place?"

Sean didn't have to think twice.

"Not tonight."

Chapter Six

THE BUILDING IN downtown Seattle was a mix of old and new. Brick exteriors from the turn of the century that had been renovated into roomy lofts with spectacular views. Owners had every amenity at their fingertips. Laundry pick-up and delivery, concierge service that with one call could provide residents with anything from late night take-out to tickets to the symphony. It was city living at its finest.

Sean walked out of the elevator and into his penthouse loft. Alone. Simone had not been happy when he dropped her off with no sex and no promise of it in the future. He knew in his heart of hearts that the days of fun and uncomplicated sex were quickly becoming a thing of the past.

It was a week before the start of training camp. This was the time to kick up his heels. When he had left the club, Gaige and Pete were doing exactly that. All over the city, his current, future, and wannabe teammates engaged in activities that would soon be frowned upon. Drinking. Late nights. Sex until dawn—and beyond.

What was he doing? Sean grabbed a bottle of water from the fridge. He was spending the night alone. Happily and without a single twinge of regret.

From his vantage point, the city stretched out in front of him—full of possibilities. Tonight he chose his couch and a good book. He blamed Riley Preston.

No. That wasn't fair. He couldn't blame Riley. This was on him. She was never around. Since her return to Seattle, Sean had seen her exactly three times. From a distance. She didn't hang out with the team or hide in the stands. This was a new Riley.

All of a sudden, he couldn't get her out of his head.

Sean flopped down onto his couch—the softer than soft one that he bought for this exact purpose. It stood alone in front of the floor to ceiling windows that dominated the west side of the room. It was his favorite place in the loft. Perfect for taking naps or simply relaxing after a long, tiring day.

At first, Sean had thought Riley was avoiding him. When he mentioned it, Gaige assured him that wasn't the case. She was busy doing everything a person had to do when they were uprooting their life from one coast to the other.

Sean understood. Still, after five years, didn't he deserve a hello? He thought back to that last series of events before Riley left Seattle. God, he had been an arrogant shit. So certain a smile and a wink could solve any problem.

Sean wasn't ready to admit that he had broken her heart. However, he had bruised it. Carelessly. He hadn't wanted her crushing on him—especially when the whole team knew about it. It was embarrassing to have a kid hanging around with stars in her eyes.

Except she hadn't been a kid. Not really. She had been a young woman. Inexperienced, yes. Also insecure and completely earnest.

Sean could see that now. Back then, all he saw was an inconvenience that needed to be dealt with as swiftly as possible. He hadn't considered his words or paid attention to her reaction. Before the conversation had finished, Sean was already planning his evening—one filled with a few drinks, a few laughs, and some great sex.

Their last meeting had been brief. Sean remembered a feeling of awkwardness. It passed quickly. Riley seemed a little subdued but friendly. Sean was convinced she was over her infatuation. He dismissed her with his usual self-centered conceit. A vague wave in her direction and he was hitting on another woman—easily conquered and quickly forgotten.

Sean had no regrets when it came to the many, many women in his past. They knew the score and he tried to make the experience as good for them as it was for him. Many of them looked for bragging rights. They wanted to join the *I slept with Sean McBride club*. And Sean was happy to oblige.

It took him a while to realize Riley was gone. A couple of weeks. Sean cringed at the memory.

"Hey, I haven't seen Riley around lately."

The team was in the locker room getting dressed. Miami and the last game of the regular season. It didn't count for anything. The Knights were headed to the playoffs as the third seed. Their only concern was to come out as healthy as they went in. The starters would play a series or two, before being pulled. No need to take any chances by playing them the entire game.

Gaige adjusted his shoulder pads, then pulled on his jersey before answering Sean's off-handed question.

"Riley isn't around because she's in Boston."

"Seems like a strange time to take a trip. She never misses a game."

"She's not coming back, Sean."

"For today's game." Sean nodded, lacing his shoe. When Gaige didn't respond, he frowned. "She *is* coming back. Right?"

"No."

"What about the team? And school?"

Gaige simply shrugged. He grabbed his helmet. Most of the team were already gathered at the far end of the room for Coach Coleman's pre-game talk.

"Gaige," Sean stopped him before he could leave. He lowered his voice even though there was no one around them to hear. "Tell me she didn't leave because of me."

"One day, Sean, you're going to wake up and realize the world does not revolve around you. Riley left because it was time to move on with her life. Away from her parents. Away from the Preston name."

Sean felt a wave of relief. With a grin, he slapped Gaige on the back.

"Good for her. I'm sure a year away will do her good."

Except it hadn't been a year. Or two. It had been five. And now she was back.

Sean hadn't spent a lot of time thinking about her. Every now and then—for no reason—he would wonder how she was doing. He knew that Gaige was in regular contact, even visiting from time to time.

Occasionally, someone like Sol or Pete would ask how Riley was doing. Gaige didn't supply very much information. The basics, nothing more. She loved Harvard. She graduated near the top of her class. No, she wasn't coming back to Seattle.

Sean lived his life. Riley lived hers. Separate and happy. At least, Sean was happy. He had to assume she was the same. Again, he didn't give it much thought.

When had that changed? Sean wondered. He was still happy enough. However, there was a mildly unsettled feeling. A discontent with the status quo. He felt as if he were waiting for something big to happen. It was only a matter of what and when.

Wondering about Riley on a regular basis had snuck up on him. That first mention of her return, almost six months ago, had started the ball rolling.

"Did you see Riley Preston?" The comment had come from Bryce Anders. The weak side safety joined the team six years ago. Just before Riley had moved to Boston.

"Preston? As in the owner?" Tony Long shoved a t-shirt into his bag. He had only been playing defensive tackle for the Knights for two years. "Is she a relative?"

"Daughter. The last time I saw her, she was this skinny thing. Her hair was always pulled back into a ponytail and she wore no makeup."

"And now?"

"Crazy good! Skinny no more. Great curves and an ass to be proud of."

"Wonder how she feels about sexy football players with tattoos?" Tony flexed his ink-covered bicep.

"I saw her first," Bryce said, giving his buddy a friendly shove.

"Maybe we can tag-team her. That redhead from Hooters loved every minute."

"Let it go." Gaige grabbed Sean's arm when he would have followed the other men as they left the locker room."

"They shouldn't talk about Riley that way. Hell, they shouldn't talk about her at all."

"It doesn't mean anything. How many times have you made comments about a random woman?"

Sean opened his mouth to protest but nothing came out. He could argue that Riley was different. But was she? The women he spoke of were someone's sister or friend or daughter. He hadn't thought of that when he bragged up his many exploits. It wasn't fair to expect his teammates to be any different. However, a little voice that he had never heard before made it clear.

This was not a random woman. This was Riley.

"You didn't tell me she was back."

"Why would I?" Gaige grabbed his bag. "You didn't show any interest while she was away. It didn't occur to me that you would care what she was up to one way or the other."

"We talk about all kinds of shit."

"Not Riley."

"I know." Sean walked out the door behind Gaige. "Why? I liked the kid. The only time you mention her is when one of the guys specifically asks."

"One of the guys. Not you. Nothing was stopping you, Sean. Unless it was guilt."

"Hey, you told me she didn't leave town because of me." Sean gave Gaige a sharp look. "Was that a lie?"

"She left for the reasons I stated. This isn't about her feelings. It's about yours. Just because there is no reason to feel guilty, doesn't mean the feeling isn't there."

"It isn't," Sean stated firmly. And he meant it—mostly. "My conscience is clear."

"Fair enough." Gaige disengaged the locks on his car. "Let's stop at *The Ridge*. All I've been able to think about for the last hour is one of their thick, juicy steaks."

Sean slid into the passenger side. His car was in the shop—as usual. It was time to give up on the vintage Jag and go with something new and shiny.

"I've been trying to cut back on red meat." Sean tried to eat healthily. Sometimes he succeeded. Sometimes he didn't. "Hell, who am I kidding. Steak it is."

"There's my man."

"About Riley."

"No." Gaige smoothly pulled into traffic.

"I—"

"Don't bother her, Sean. If Riley wants to see you, she will. You haven't given her a second thought in five years. Now is not the time to change that."

As it turned out, that was easier said than done. The proverbial Genie was out of the bottle and there wasn't any putting it back.

Sean closed his eyes. He felt dead tired but his brain wouldn't shut down. Rolling off the couch, he walked to where his phone was plugged. The illuminated dial read one thirty-five. Not too late to call up Simone. With a little charm and a properly worded apology, she might be willing to let him make a booty call.

He waited for his body to respond. Nope. His dick lay as dormant as a bear in winter. Not even a twitch of interest. Sean pulled up a picture. His current favorite. One look and his dick sprang to attention.

Riley.

He had downloaded the shot from a gossip site. The article had hinted—in very broad strokes—that she was smiling at a certain cyber-billionaire who had made his money in his twenties and, in his thirties, retired to the good life. Sean recognized the name. Was that Riley's type? Brains over brawn?

Unconsciously, Sean rolled his head, the muscles in his back flexing. With one more look at Riley's sparkling blue eyes and dark hair. Had it aways been shot with streaks of red?

Sean entered his bathroom. Before he moved into the loft, he had the entire place gutted and redecorated to his specifications. That included a shower big enough to fit four adults. In his hedonistic imagination, he pictured himself and one, two, or three lovely ladies playing water games of the best kind. Lather, fuck, repeat.

The reality had been more PG than triple-X. He had been living here for almost a year and the only action his shower had seen was Sean giving himself a helping hand.

It didn't take him long to weigh his options. Toss and turn all night or take care of his most immediate problem. Sean needed help. When he had to debate himself on the merits of masturbation, he knew he was in trouble.

Leaning a hand against the marble tile, he hit the soap dispenser with the other. The lemon scent hit him as he closed his eyes and spread his legs. He groaned with relief, his strokes long and slow. He could picture another hand. Smaller. Softer. It made his breath quicken when he imagined another body close to his. The fantasy didn't last. It never did. Just long enough for him to reach his peak and call out her name.

Riley.

Chapter Seven

"HOW DO THEY look, Coach?"

"You know me, Riley. I'm cautiously optimistic."

Harry Coleman smiled at her, his face lined from years of experience and exposure to the elements. The life of a head coach wasn't easy on the skin—or the digestion—but it was his life. And he loved every second.

"Which is exactly what you said at your press conference this morning. Tell me what you didn't tell them."

"If Logan Price's knee holds up, we'll field the best team I've had with the Knights."

"Gaige's pet project is working out?"

When Logan Price hurt his knee during his rookie year, it was a long shot he would ever play again. Watching him out on the field, running with ease—the joy of a little boy shining on his face—was a sight to see. She was happy for him. And thrilled for the team.

"Don't play coy," Harry scoffed. "I don't know what you said to put that in motion, but thank you. This could be our year."

That was what Riley wanted to hear. She knew they looked good. The talent was there—so was the dedication. They were hungry for a championship. As were the other thirty-one NFL teams. Between now and February, there would be plenty of ups and downs. Injuries.

Arguments. A few flat out tantrums. It was Harry's job to deal with the problems once the season started.

Riley hoped that management had given him the tools to get them to the top of the mountain. They were champions. *On paper.* However, no one handed you a trophy in September. To be the last team standing, they had to pull it all together when it mattered most.

Pulling a few strings from the other side of the country hadn't been easy. Riley had encouraged the team to draft Mikhail Branch. He was a tough center with nerves of steel and could snap the ball with pinpoint accuracy. He protected Gaige like a favorite son. The two had made the Pro Bowl three years straight.

"Denver looks tough this year." The Knights kicked the season off against the Broncos.

"Every team is tough." Harry shot her a look and laughed. "It's the NFL."

"Any given Sunday," Riley grinned. It was a cliché for a reason. No matter the record or the personnel, you had to play the game. Upsets happened all the time.

"Any given Sunday," Harry chimed back.

It was Tuesday. Riley felt as though she was a little girl waiting for Christmas. It seemed like game day would never get here.

Five years. It was a long time to go without something you loved so much. Riley could have gone to games on the East Coast, but it would have felt like cheating. She had watched the Knights on TV, determined that the next time she watched them live, it would be in Seattle.

Now that the day drew close, she felt a stirring of nerves. If this kept up, come Sunday, she would be a mess.

"I'll see you tonight?"

"I haven't missed a kick-off party in twenty years," Harry stated. "My wife buys a new dress every year."

"And what do you buy, Harry?"

Harry Coleman was notorious for owning two suits. One for weddings, one for funerals. As far as he was concerned, if you were going to wear a tie, the moment better be a big one.

"New underwear," he quipped.

"Okay." Smiling, Riley shook her head. Lord, she had missed this man. "I'm sorry I asked. Some things should remain a mystery."

"Never look behind the curtain, little girl. The wizard is never what he seems."

With those prophetic words, Harry Coleman blew his whistle, officially calling an end to the practice.

"Riley."

Gaige jogged over. His face was flushed and his blond hair matted with sweat. He was sexy as hell. Some would say she was an idiot for not falling for him. Riley would say she had nothing to do with it. She was happy to say that her heart, or whatever determined such things, was immune to the potent charms of Mr. Gaige Benson.

Riley loved him unreservedly—as a friend. Gaige was a layer of bedrock she knew she could always count on for support. Romantic love fogged the brain and screwed things up. She knew that from bitter experience.

"You look fresh as a daisy."

"And you look like you've been run ragged. Those new recruits too much for you?"

"The day I can't outmaneuver a few rookies is the day I hang up my cleats." He winked, his green eyes twinkling with humor. "One more season."

"Don't remind me." Unconcerned about putting her clean blouse against his dirty jersey, Riley hugged him tight. "I want you to change your mind."

"Time passes, Riley." Gaige gently kissed her brow. "The first time I threw a spiral, you couldn't pronounce the word football."

"Don't give me that *I'm an old man* routine. You made those twenty-somethings eat your dust today."

"Experience only trumps enthusiasm for so long. By the end of the season, those rookies will be mowing down rival QBs."

"Then we'll be glad they're on our side."

"Every side has them."

Gaige had been dodging them for years with varying degrees of success. The chances of one of those eager puppies causing him major damage increased every year. He planned on getting out while his body, and his mind, were still in decent working order.

This year was it. Win or lose. The affable glint left his eyes, replaced by steel and determination. Losing wasn't an option. Gaige Benson was going out a winner if it meant kicking every ass between him and the Super Bowl.

"You've done your part to get me to the top of the mountain," he said, squeezing her affectionately. "The rest is up to those fifty-two lunkheads and me to do the rest. And here comes lunkhead number one."

When she tried to pull away, Gaige tightened his hold. "Stay put," he whispered. "It won't hurt Sean to think you're interested."

"In you?" Riley almost giggled—and she never giggled. After six months of playing peek-a-boo with Sean, she thought she was ready to meet him up close and personal. So why did she want to hide? *Not today*, she thought. *Tomorrow. Next week. Next year. Anytime but now.*

"Watch the smartass comments or I'll disappear. You want to be alone with Sean?"

Riley zipped her lip. She needed a buffer. Gaige's big, solidly built body would do nicely.

"I was hoping to finally get a chance to say welcome back. Or should I say, welcome home, Riley."

Sean's voice sent a shiver up her spine. She wasn't looking at him and her reaction was everything she hoped it wouldn't be. Breathing deeply, Riley shifted, leaving Gaige's arm around her shoulders.

One look was all it took to realize it was easier to lie to herself at a distance. She could tell herself that a man was out of her blood. However, when that blood heated at the sound of her name on his lips, it was time for some hardball honesty.

Three thousand miles and five years hadn't changed her feelings. Her ability to hide it was another matter. Relaxing her grip on Gaige's waist, Riley greeted Sean with a friendly smile. Warm. Impersonal.

And fake as a three-dollar bill.

"Thank you, Sean."

Riley's smile widened. *Careful. Too wide looks forced. Tone it down a bit.*

"I would have said something sooner but we always seem to miss each other."

"Busy lives. Neither of us has very much free time." Riley shrugged.

"Ships that pass in the night," Gaige said with seeming innocence.

Surreptitiously, Riley pinched his leg. Now who was being the smartass?

"Can you hang around until I grab a shower?" Sean knew something was going on. Riley was twitchy and Gaige looked like he wanted to burst out laughing. "I'll buy you a cup of coffee and we can catch up."

"That sounds great, Sean. Really."

"Really?"

This time, Gaige's comment earned him a harder pinch. On the ass.

"Okay." Gaige's voice rose an octave. He dropped his arm, moving out of Riley's range. "If we're going to hit that party, we need to get a move on."

"The party?"

It had slipped Sean's mind. When Riley arrived toward the end of practice, he became entirely focused on her. He missed the last pass Gaige sent his way, the ball sailing through his fingers. It had earned him a dirty look from his QB and a few catcalls from the guys.

One would have thought, with so long to think about it, Sean would have known what he wanted to say. As he approached Riley, he couldn't think of a single thing. She looked fresh and sweet. A sharp contrast to the man she had her arms around.

Gaige was sweaty, dirty, and the way Riley plastered herself to him, it didn't bother her one bit. Were they more than friends? Sean had never thought so before now.

As he jogged over, he tried to look at them objectively. A man. A woman. Hugging. Innocent. Then Gaige kissed Riley's forehead and Sean couldn't help himself.

What other parts of Riley's body had his old friend kissed?

"I don't want to hold you up." Riley smiled at him. She reached over and briefly clasped his arm. "We'll catch up later."

"At the party?" Sean almost grabbed her hand, forcing her to maintain contact. "I can dazzle you with my dance moves."

"Sure. Why not."

"Don't forget."

Sean felt awkward. Like a teenager with his first crush. He had never felt this way—not even when he *was* a teenager.

"Jesus," Gaige muttered under his breath.

Sean noticed Gaige's *you have to be shitting me* look. If he were prone to blushing, now would have been the time.

Sean cleared his throat. "See you later, Riley."

"Did you know?" Riley asked Gaige when Sean was out of earshot.

"What?"

Gaige sighed. Now he was supposed to be a mind reader. All he wanted was a shower, some downtime with his teammates and a glass or two of top shelf whiskey. Was that too much to ask?

"That I'm still in love with Sean."

"I suspected. It was up to you to decide. Nothing I said would have mattered."

"You could have mentioned it."

"Would you have wanted to hear it?"

"No."

"Then…"

"I've been living in a dream world." Riley knocked the heel of her hand against her forehead. "So much for older and wiser. Maybe it's just sex."

"Maybe." Gaige almost laughed at the comically hopeful expression on her face.

"Should I sleep with him? Get it out of my system?"

"If you do? Don't tell me about it."

Gaige didn't want to know about Riley's sex life—especially when he knew so much about Sean's. He had known, when she decided to leave Boston for Seattle, there was a strong possibility Sean's perspective regarding Riley would change. Time and distance had a way of doing that.

Riley had always been beautiful. Gangly legs, messy hair, and all. Now she was stunning. A blind man would have noticed. And Sean was not blind to women. Especially when they looked like Riley.

"He is interested. Right?" Riley shot Gaige an embarrassed look. "Don't say it. I'm acting like a girl."

"Yes," Gaige nodded. Then to temper his annoyance, he winked. "You're allowed some hormonal backtracking, Riley. Don't beat yourself up over it."

"You're a good friend, Gaige. To both Sean and me."

"Which means I am officially benching myself. I will now be a casual observer firmly entrenched on the sidelines. You and Sean are on your own."

"Which means we're bound to make a mess of it." Riley's smile conveyed a touch of humor. Inside, she was a bundle of uncertainty.

"What can I say? I have faith you'll work it out. One way or another." Gaige walked with her across the field, stopping at the exit.

"One way or another? You make it sound so simple."

"Life isn't simple, Riley. As for love? Beats me. I've never fallen."

"Why not? Why hasn't Gaige Benson lost his heart to some lucky lady?"

Gaige was the most together person Riley knew. His personal life was a mystery because he chose to keep it that way. The pictures of him and his woman of the moment filled page after page on any internet search.

However, he didn't carry the same reputation as Sean. They called Gaige the *Gentleman Lover*—a moniker he hated—because he managed the seemingly impossible task of leaving his women happy. No fits of jealousy, no broken hearts. Riley imagined there had to be the exception, but no one who had dated Gaige spoke ill of him to the press. In this day and age, that was impressive.

Gaige had lovers and playmates and friends. What he didn't have was love. Unless…

"Are you pining for an unrequited love?" Riley reached for his hand, ready to give comfort. After years of leaning on him, she wanted to return the favor.

"Pining? Unrequited?" Gaige shook his head, his green eyes filled with laughter. "No and no, Riley. My heart is untouched and unbroken."

"Never a twinge?"

"No."

Riley had a million questions. And she kept them all to herself. She knew Gaige. The look on his face said that this subject was closed. She wouldn't push because she respected his privacy. If the day came that he wanted to open up, she was always here. She wasn't going anywhere.

"See you at the party?" Riley returned Gaige's grateful smile, letting him know she understood that the change of subject was appreciated.

"I'll be there."

"Are you bringing a date?"

Gaige laughed, his easy good humor restored. "Don't I always?" With that simple yet telling response, he turned and walked toward the locker room.

"Aren't you afraid the well of new women will run dry?" Riley called out after him.

"That's just it," he called over his shoulder. "How can I settle for one when there is a never-ending supply?"

A never-ending supply.

The words stuck with Riley as she drove away from the stadium. Gaige was looking forty in the eye and he was still a major player. What made her think Sean was ready to settle for one woman?

What made Riley think that woman would be her?

Sean was interested. Gaige had said as much—and Riley had learned to figure out when a man wanted her. Would it be enough? If Sean was only interested in an affair, was Riley ready to turn away? Or would she embrace the chance to have him—on any terms?

Tonight was the first step in finding the answers to her questions. This was the debut of the new Riley.

It was time to find out if she was dealing with the same old Sean.

Chapter Eight

CORRINE PRESTON ENJOYED hosting the yearly kick-off party for the Knights.

She didn't give a damn about football. It was the main subject of conversation. Defense. Offense. Salary caps. Injuries.

Ugh!.

Corrine smiled through the inane chatter, tuning out the voices. Her pleasure didn't come from the game; it came from the players. Eye candy. Young men in the prime of their lives. Fit and fabulous.

The guest list was carefully assembled. The team—naturally. Coaches and trainers. The Knights' board of directors. Girlfriends and wives were a necessary evil. The older she got, the younger the other women became. However, with the help of good genes and a discreet plastic surgeon, Corrine fought Mother Nature at every turn. For now, she was winning the battle.

Circulating through the crowd, Corrine scoped out the new meat. Mmm. There was nothing better than a young, malleable lover. From birth, her life had been ruled by powerful men. First her father, then her husband. She liked to be in charge in the bedroom. It was one of the few places she had complete control.

The room was filled with past conquests, potential new ones and, much to her chagrin, a few failures. Corrine hated rejection. She never made a move unless she was certain of the outcome.

Her first mistake had been Gaige Benson. She took one look at his blond hair and green eyes coupled with a body made for giving her pleasure, and Corrine couldn't see anything else. She was shocked when he turned her down. Her first reaction had been to get him traded. Gerald laughed at the suggestion.

"Benson is a franchise quarterback. The Knights are not letting him go."

"But he…" Corrine hesitated. She and her husband had an open marriage. However, that didn't mean they discussed their lovers.

"Suck it up, Corrine." Gerald knew his wife's penchant for young football players. He approved of anything that kept her out of his hair. She could screw the whole team and staff for all he cared. Still, it amused him to see her bent out of shape over a rare miss. "You hit on the wrong man. As shocking as it may be, not everyone finds you irresistible."

Corrine suffered the humiliation. It was a bitter pill to swallow. However, Gaige Benson was only one man. One mistake. Her *only* mistake. Until Sean McBride.

She blamed Riley. Corrine's interest in Sean had been minor. He had too much experience for her taste. However, when she saw the opportunity to take a taste *and* rub her daughter's holier than thou nose in it, she couldn't resist.

The backfire had been instantaneous and painful. The look of disgust on Sean's face after she playfully squeezed his chest was bad enough. Riley's reaction was a blow she felt to this day.

Lord, it had felt good to slap that smug little bitch's face. She should have done it sooner. Corrine had hoped for tears and recriminations. Instead, Riley threatened her. *Her.* It had been unthinkable. Unpalatable. For five years, the need for revenge had simmered in Corrine's mind. *One day*, she promised herself.

That was for another time. She looked forward to this night every year. She planned on enjoying being the most beautiful and desirable woman in the room. Fluffing her freshly highlighted hair, Corrine entered the room. The smile that was meant to be seductive froze on her lips when the first thing she saw was a beautiful young woman surrounded by men. *Her* men.

It had been five years. The changes in her appearance were startling. However, Corrine recognized the brunette in the cherry red dress immediately.

Riley.

Her daughter was the laughing, sparkling center of attention. The men grinned and fawned over her like anxious puppies. Corrine's eyes narrowed. Her face grew hot. It was all she could do not to stomp her foot in frustration. She had money and beauty. She was always the belle of this ball. The hostess with the mostess. This was her territory and she would not stand by and let her place be usurped.

"She looks good, doesn't she?"

Corrine jumped. She hadn't heard anyone approach. She could see Gerald out of the corner of her eye, but her attention stayed fixed on Riley.

"I suppose."

"It's amazing what a few years and some polish will do. Neither of us realized our daughter had been such a diamond in the rough."

"Can the faux pride, Daddy." Corrine's voice dripped the kind of sarcasm reserved for her husband. "You don't like her reappearance any more than I do," she added with a sneer. "If you were any kind of a man, you would have given me a son."

"You think a son would have made you happy?" Gerald tried picturing it. The kid would have turned out one of two ways. A sniveling mama's boy, or a sociopath who would snap, killing them in their sleep. He had no paternal love for Riley, but a least he didn't worry about her giving him a shotgun blast to the head.

Then, because this was Corrine and he couldn't resist one more jab, he said, "Are you certain she's mine?"

"You asked me that twenty-five years ago." Until Riley had been born, Corrine hadn't been sure of the answer. "Look at her. She's you in a skirt. And without the five o'clock shadow." She ran a hand over his bristly cheek. "Your latest trollop must like the unkempt look. You are such a slave to your dick."

Gerald captured Corinne's wrist, his grip tighter than necessary. "Let's sheath the claws and work together. Unless you like Riley's newfound popularity."

"What can you do?" Corrine was open to anything that would pop Riley's balloon.

"God, you're bloodthirsty." Gerald recognized the look in Corrine's eyes. Dangerous and potentially lethal. It had made her exciting when they were first married. Then, like all women, she grew tiresome. Now, he could use it to his advantage.

"This," Gerald motioned around the room, "is her biggest weakness. She loves the team."

"Ruin them." Corrine could find new playmates. "You should have done it years ago."

"There are too many checks and balances in place." Gerald had tried to get around his father's convoluted will—it hadn't worked. "I've kept this team a middle of the pack non-contender. Riley wants to change that."

"Can she?"

"Yes." Gerald hated to admit it, but it was true. Riley had her grandfather's savvy and business sense. Combined with her love for the game, it was exactly what the Knights had been missing.

"I can't ruin the Knights." Gerald watched Riley place a friendly hand on Gaige Benson's arm. "However, I can make life very uncomfortable for our daughter. By mid-season, she'll be happy to leave town."

"I liked her in Boston."

"Liked?"

"Fine. I *preferred* when she was three thousand miles away. Whatever you need, Gerald. I'm in."

"When was the last time we worked on something together?"

Riley's laughter rang out. Happy. Carefree. There wasn't room in

Seattle for two Preston women. Especially when one of them was younger and cosmetic surgery free.

"About twenty-five years ago."

"WILL IT MAKE you uncomfortable if I admit to having a bit of a girl crush? If we weren't the same age, I would want to grow up to be you."

"Me? You are a tough-ass business woman. *I* want to be *you*."

Riley smiled at Claire Thornton. They wore dueling four-inch heels. Riley's put her a shade over five feet nine. Claire's had her topping six feet. The blond was slim and athletic with killer legs and blue eyes the color of a cloudless day. Had Riley said *girl crush*? She was one step away from wishing she swung both ways.

It was an interesting situation. Riley knew Claire through Gaige. The women had spoken on the phone, but this was their first face to face meeting.

Riley had been a little nervous. Her temper was still simmering. Claire had been up for the assistant trainer's job. It was her dream—a goal she had worked her ass off to obtain. Then, just when she thought the job was hers, it had been pulled out from under her. Boom. Thanks for playing, but no cigar.

"I wish I could have changed their minds, Claire."

Claire shrugged with a half-smile. "Football is a man's game—on and off the field. I should have known the owners wouldn't want a woman treating their athletes. Things change. But it is a slow and arduous process. A woman will get there, it just won't be me."

It was true. However, it didn't make Riley happy. Outraged, she hadn't taken her fight to her father. This time, she went to a man who judged people on their abilities, not their gender.

Ross Morrisey was a minority owner in the Knights. He also ran a very successful sporting goods business based out of the Northwest. He had given Riley's fledgling consulting firm a chance, making them both a lot of money. She thought if she could get Ross on her side, she would rally the other owners and get Claire the job she deserved.

Riley hated to fail, but there was no budging Ross or anyone else.

No one would come right out and say it, but they were not going to hire a woman. No matter how qualified she was.

"Let it go, Riley. I have."

"Really?"

"No." Claire laughed. The fact that she could, said a lot. Last week a smile was beyond her abilities. "But I'm getting there. It helps to have someone special in my corner."

"Gaige?" Riley's smile turned sly. "Or Logan?"

"Both." Almost to herself, she said, "Gaige's misfits."

"Excuse me?"

"Gaige has a way of collecting people in need. He gave me a boost when I was at the end of my rope. Logan had given up on ever playing football again. Who knows how many others he has helped over the years."

"Misfits." Riley supposed she could add herself to the club. "You might want to keep that to yourself."

"He loves to help but hates to be thanked," Claire agreed. "Our Gaige is a complicated man."

"Whatever makes him tick, we are very lucky to have him in our lives."

"Amen."

"Now that we are halfway to BFFs." Riley grinned, tapping her wine glass against Claire's. "It must have felt good to arrive with Logan. A few weeks ago you two were still hiding your relationship."

"Keeping it on the down low wasn't easy." Claire loved that she didn't have to look around in case anyone was listening. "Until we knew if I got the job with the Knights, I was Logan's physical therapist. Period."

Other than Gaige, Riley was the only one who had known the truth.

When Gaige went to Oklahoma to see Logan Price, he took Claire Thornton with him. Claire had some radical ideas about rehabbing sports injuries. She stayed with Logan, getting him ready for his comeback. Gaige was tickled to death that the pair had fallen in love.

However, Claire had wanted the assistant trainer's job with the

Knights. They decided it would be best if she and Logan didn't advertise just how close they had become. If Claire wanted to get her foot in the door, being a player's girlfriend wouldn't be an asset.

In the end, it hadn't mattered.

Claire didn't have the job, but she had Logan—and understood that she had come out a winner.

"About those ointments and potions you've developed?" Claire had her own concoctions that she used to help an athlete's aches and pains. She had used them on Logan. If he were any example, they had worked wonders.

"What about them?" Claire took a salmon puff off the tray of the circulating waiter.

"I want to help you get them on the market."

"Really?" Claire almost choked on the puff.

"Careful." Laughing, Riley gently patted her on the back. "If I do my job properly, and I always do, those magic elixirs are going to make you a rich woman. You want to be around to enjoy it."

"Riley. I don't know what to say."

"We'll hash the details out, then you can say yes." Riley loved that she was in a position to do something for Claire. "The deal will be more than fair."

"I'm sure."

"Don't be. Get a lawyer. Gaige will give you the name of a good one. Read everything. Twice. If you don't understand something, ask questions."

"Are you planning on cheating me?"

"No. But I won't be the last person you deal with. There are a lot of people who wouldn't blink if it meant making an extra buck."

"Thank you, Riley. I know there's more I want to say, but right now I'm a little overwhelmed."

Understanding, Riley changed the subject.

"One more week and the games count." Riley looked to where Gaige and Logan were speaking with Sol Bellows and Pete Jacobs. "Logan has looked great in pre-season. You've done wonders, Claire."

"He has worked his ass off." Claire beamed with pride. And love. She and Logan could try to hide it, but anyone with eyes could tell how they felt.

"Is he nervous?"

"Sure. In a good way." Claire took a sip of her drink. "I'm the one who can't sleep. As much as I hated it, I would go back to waiting tables if it meant Logan could play football again."

No doubt about it, Riley thought. Claire Thornton and Logan Price had the real thing. Love with a capital L. It made her long for the same—with a certain someone who might never feel the same.

"Speak of the devil."

"Is that what we were doing?" Following the path of Riley's gaze, Claire nodded. "Ah. I see. Sean McBride. He certainly flirts like the devil. If I weren't off the market, I would have been tempted to give that man a ride. Oops. Did I hit a nerve?"

"It's an old one. Why it hasn't toughened up by now, I don't know."

"Don't you?"

Sean chose that moment to meet Riley's gaze. She was used to the jump of her heartbeat and the flutter in the stomach. However, this was something new. It was what she saw in his eyes that made her skin tingle with thousands of tiny electric jolts. She hadn't changed. *Sean* had. He wasn't looking at her with the old amused indulgence. He saw a woman. And he wanted her.

"It isn't fair. He's already gorgeous. In a suit and tie and freshly shaven. I'll bet he smells like heaven."

Riley's eyes widened. She hadn't meant to say that aloud. How embarrassing.

Hiding her smile, Claire graciously gave Riley a break. "I'm going to leave you before Sean gets here. Lunch. Next week. You pick the day and place, I'll be there." Claire clinked their glasses one more time. "Good luck."

"I like her."

Taking a breath, Riley smiled. Not the fake one she used when trying to hide her feelings. This was genuine. Welcoming. Tinged with a few nerves.

"Me too." Riley's smile widened into a grin. "So you hit on her?"

"I did not!"

Riley believed him. Sean's flirting was automatic. When he was serious, he turned it up to another level. Claire had encountered the watered down version that every breathing female received when in Sean's orbit. Like breathing in and out, Sean flirted.

It drove the old Riley crazy with jealousy. The new Riley thought it was charmingly harmless. Wow! She had changed.

"It doesn't matter, Sean."

"It doesn't?" Sean frowned.

"Nope. We're friends. Right? Friends don't judge."

"I want to be your friend, Riley."

And more. So much more.

Sean hadn't been able to take his eyes off Riley all evening. She glowed. Her halo of dark hair flowed around her creamy shoulders. Her lips were red. Not bright. Like the cherries he gorged himself on every summer. The color was echoed in the dress that swirled around her legs when she walked. The little straps that crisscrossed her back looked delicate—easily broken. One pull and he could have the material pooling at her feet.

What was Riley wearing under her dress? Not a bra. As her chest rose and fell with each breath, Sean could see the swell of her breasts. Not too big. Not too small. Sean wondered if the tips tasted as sweet as cherries. He couldn't wait to find out.

"Up here, buster." Riley snapped her fingers in front of Sean's face. "What are you? Twelve? Haven't you learned not to stare at a woman's breasts in public?"

"Not staring. Imagining."

"I don't want to know."

"Are you sure?" Sean's lips curved. Flirting with Riley was a new and heady experience. "I wonder how turned on I could get us by using only words?"

"You? I doubt it takes much. I'm not that easy."

"Wanna bet?"

Sean saw the spark of interest in Riley's eyes and he knew he had her.

"Lay out the terms."

"Nothing complicated. We stay where we are. Surrounded by people. Sipping our drinks."

"And?"

"I talk to you."

"And," Riley urged.

Sean hadn't said anything out of the ordinary. However, his voice had dropped, enveloping them in a cloud of intimacy their location belied.

"I want to kiss you, Riley." Sean spoke the words with little inflection. He could see the way Riley's pupils dilated. She felt them. Deeply. "Not on the lips. Not yet. There's a spot. The curve of your neck. I'll breathe in your scent." Sean inhaled. "Sweet. Spicy. When I taste you, there will be the faintest trace of salt. It's a combination that drives me crazy."

"Wait." Riley took a deep breath. "If this is a bet, what is the wager?"

"If I win?" Sean smiled over the rim of his glass. "You let me take you out to dinner."

"A date?" Riley asked in surprise. That wasn't what she had expected. "What else?"

"That will be up to you."

"And if I win?"

"Name it."

Riley tipped her head to the side, considering her options. The list was endless. Naked Sean vacuuming her floors. Cooking her breakfast. Scrubbing her back. Every thought involved Sean without a stitch of clothing. Tempting. But too soon.

"Two dates."

Sean smiled. "Dinner and dancing."

"You dance?"

"It's all about rhythm. Whether you're running a route during a game, or guiding a beautiful woman around the dance floor. Or…"

"Or?" Riley waited expectantly.

"Making love."

Not sex. Love. Had the difference been deliberate? Did Sean realize what he had done? Riley couldn't be certain. However, *she* knew. Her heartbeat kicked up another notch.

"I'm not a virgin."

"I didn't ask."

"I thought you should know. I didn't wait for you, Sean."

"How screwed up would that have been?" Sean shuddered at the thought. "A modern day Miss Havisham."

Riley laughed. "Without the dilapidated mansion and ratty wedding dress."

"I haven't been a saint, Riley."

"You haven't?" Riley gasped in mock outrage.

"The future is—"

Riley quickly interrupted him.

"I wouldn't want to know if I could, Sean. Our past is a bit odd. Our future is blissfully unknown. I vote we concentrate on the here and now. I want to get to know you. Woman to man. Friends. Maybe lovers. The rest we'll play by ear."

"You have grown up, Riley."

"Have you?"

"You'll have to determine that for yourself."

That alone was proof Sean wasn't the man-child she used to know. He didn't make a bold, sweeping statement professing his newfound maturity. Riley liked this Sean. And she was going to enjoy getting to know him.

"I hope you haven't changed completely." Riley gave Sean a provocative smile. "We had a bet. Remember? The old Sean wouldn't let that slip by."

"No, he wouldn't." Sean's voice lowered. "There's nothing wrong with mixing a bit of old with the new."

"I couldn't agree more."

"Good." The flecks of green in Sean's hazel eyes sparkled with mischief. "Now, where was I? Oh, that's right. I was tasting you."

"Do I get to return the favor?"

"Sweetheart. I wouldn't have it any other way."

Satisfied with his answer, Riley kept her eyes on Sean's, listening with rapt attention. It didn't take him long to win the bet. Or was she the winner? Considering the stakes, Riley had no problem calling it a draw.

Chapter Nine

RILEY FELL ONTO her bed with a sigh, the material of her quilt cushioning her like a soft, downy pillow.

Laughing, Riley rolled around. She was happy. The happiest she had been in a long time. It was amazing what some sexy talk and a kiss could do for a woman's spirits.

Riley lifted her fingers to her mouth. It had been an hour, yet she could still feel Sean's lips pressed against her own. He had tasted like whiskey and something heady. Like Sean. Elusive, yet oh so tantalizing. You knew it might not be good for you, but you couldn't resist sampling it again. And again.

Unlike the first time she kissed Sean—Riley cringed when she remembered throwing herself at him that afternoon five years ago—this one hadn't been planned.

A fact that had made it so much more satisfying.

Flustered, in a good way, Riley excused herself to use the bathroom. She needed a few moments alone to cool down and regain her perspective. She was ready to toss caution to the wind and invite Sean home. Bad idea. Too much, too soon. Instead, she tossed cold water on her face and freshened her lip-gloss.

She knew the woman in the mirror. She was strong and

independent. She didn't need Sean to make her life better—but, man, did she want him. Riley knew what she was going to do. There had never been a choice. Not really. She was going to take a chance on Sean and herself.

This wasn't a case of jumping blind. Her eyes were open to the risks. It was worth it—because she believed the rewards would make it worthwhile.

Winking at herself, Riley left the bathroom with a bounce in her step. She was almost to the ballroom when someone grabbed her arm.

"It's me," Sean whispered, barely blocking Riley's fist.

"Sean! You scared the wits out of me."

"Good reflexes." Keeping hold of her, Sean pulled Riley to a dark alcove. "I need you alone."

"Why?" Riley had no objection. It wasn't difficult to figure out what Sean had in mind, but she wanted to hear him say the words.

"One kiss. Please, Riley." Sean backed her against the wall. Even in heels, she had to tip her head to look into his eyes. "I won't ask for anything more. Not tonight. Just. One. Kiss."

"Will you walk away if I say no?"

"You know I will."

That was all she needed to hear.

"I'm not saying no."

"Thank God."

It wasn't her first kiss. It wasn't even her first kiss with Sean. However, Riley knew this one would mean more than any of the others put together. He wanted it as much a she did.

They were equals. Riley was no longer an inexperienced young woman desperate to be loved. Sean was older, more stable. Less inclined to look past his current lover in search of his next conquest.

Unconsciously, Riley licked her lips.

"Do that again," Sean hissed, his breath whispering across her face.

"This?"

Sean's eyes followed the path of her tongue. "What do you taste like?"

"Mint and strawberries."

"How?"

"Lip-gloss and toothpaste."

With a groan, Sean closed the distance between them, his mouth covering hers. This was no tentative, getting to know you, kiss. Sean meant business. His tongue played with hers, gentle at first, then aggressive. He took charge and Riley was happy to follow his lead.

"I love strawberries." He bit her bottom lip, then bathed it with a gentle swipe. "And mint. Does the rest of you taste this sweet?"

"You'll have to wait and find out."

Riley didn't know how she formed the words. What Sean did to her mind—her body—should have been illegal. If they were, she was ready to be the first in line to break the law. This was only foreplay, and she was sinking into a pool of bliss so deep she didn't care if she ever saw daylight again.

"I'm going to touch you."

"Damn right you are."

Kissing her neck, Sean chuckled, the vibration from his lips sending jolts through her body. *That was new.* Riley was about to ask him to do it again when his hand closed over her breast. Thoughts of laughter and kisses zipped out of her brain. Her senses were concentrated on his thumb rubbing her nipple to a hard, aching peak.

"The second I saw you in this dress I wanted to rip it off and see what you are hiding underneath. No bra." Sean sighed into her ear. "I was right."

"I'm fortunate not to need one."

"I'm the fortunate one." He cupped her in his hand, squeezing gently. "Perfect fit."

"Sean." Riley's head fell back against the wall. "This is fast."

"Too fast?"

"Yes. No." She couldn't think. Not with his mouth and hand conspiring to turn her brain to mush. "Maybe?"

"I'll be good. Just let me…"

The hand not teasing her breast slipped under Riley's skirt.

"This is being good." *Oh, God*, she thought when he caressed her thigh. *This is very good.*

"Your skin is like warm silk. I want you draped over me, exhausted. Satisfied. Rubbing against me like a sweet, happy kitten."

"I'm not a cat." Riley slid her fingers through Sean's hair. "But I do have claws."

"Ouch." Sean pulled back when her fingernails bit into his scalp. "Didn't like the kitten reference? I'll remember that."

"Remember this. I'm not weak or malleable. If we have sex, it will be as equals."

"No, tie me up, tie me down fun and games?" Sean teased.

"I didn't say that."

The look Sean gave her was filled with surprise—and interest. He hadn't expected that? Good. Riley didn't want to be what he expected. She planned on keeping him on his toes.

"No more pussy cat references." Sean crossed his heart. Pulling Riley close, he wrapped both arms around her waist. With ease, he lifted her until they were eye to eye. "Now. Tell me? How kinky? Do you like to be tied up? Spanked? Let me know. I'll be happy to play master."

"Another time." With a quick, hard kiss, Riley reluctantly slid from Sean's embrace. Walking away, she said without a backward glance, "And who says *you* get to be in charge?"

"Mistress?" Sean called out, his voice squeaking.

Smiling, Riley kept on walking.

SEAN STOOD ON the sidelines, waiting to get in the game.

"Defense is going to hold. Three and out. Are you ready?"

"Worry about yourself, old man. I'm always ready."

Nodding his head, Gaige moved to the next player. It was a yearly routine. The first game of the season, their QB went from man to man, asking the same question, looking for the same answer. Sean wondered what would happen if one of the guys said he wasn't ready. Gaige already vibrated with pent up energy. The poor idiot wouldn't know what hit him.

Fortunately, this team was focused. When Gaige asked them something, they responded. Correctly.

This was Sean's eighth season. Eight! How had that happened? The time had flown by in a wink. He was at that point in his career where he appreciated every snap of the ball. He understood, the way a rookie never could, that each play could be his last.

Sean no longer played with wild abandon. However, the joy was stronger than ever. He loved his job. The knowledge that it could be taken from him at any moment made each game, each catch, all the sweeter.

"That's it," Gaige yelled. "Our ball. Let's make it count."

Sean grabbed his helmet, following Gaige onto the field. Hell yes, he would make it count. Today and every day he was lucky enough to play professional football.

"I DON'T KNOW if I can do this." Claire gripped the sides of her seat.

"Take a deep breath. After a few plays, you'll be fine." Riley patted Claire's shoulder.

"Why didn't I stay at home? I could be working out. I wouldn't have looked at the game until it was over."

"You would have been checking in every thirty seconds."

"Oh, my God. Here comes the offense. I can't look." Claire peeked through her closed eyelids. "They won't start with a running play. Don't start with a running play." When Gaige threw a quick swing pass to Sean, Claire erupted. "Why the hell didn't they start with a running play? Don't they trust Logan?"

"Calm down."

As she gave the advice, Riley did an internal happy dance. Sean ran for a twenty-yard gain. He looked good. Damn good.

Riley looked around. She had used her clout to get them seats in the sold-out crowd. The owners' suite would be filled to overflowing. A lot of business talk and back-slapping. Plus her father. No, thank you. Riley preferred it down here with the noisy fans.

Cheers erupted. Claire grabbed Riley's hand, her grip alarmingly strong.

"Did you see? Did you? Logan gained fifteen yards." Claire threw her arms up in the air. "Holy, crap. Fifteen freaking yards."

Laughing, Riley surreptitiously tested her fingers. No breaks.

"Again, Claire. Calm down. If you keep this up, you won't have enough strength to walk out of the stadium. And trust me. I'm not carrying you."

"I love that man." Claire grinned, high-fiving random strangers. "That's right. Number twenty-eight. The one with the cute ass. Logan Price is my man."

"Honey, they all got cute asses." A woman dressed from head to toe in blue and gold winked at Claire. "But Logan Price? Good for you. Tell him we're excited to have him back."

"Will do," Claire beamed.

By the end of the game, the crowd cheered Logan's name. He was back all right. With a vengeance. It wasn't necessary for Riley to carry Claire out. Her friend practically floated.

"Did you see that last run?" Claire couldn't stop talking. About the game. About Logan. About the amazing hot dogs. The subject jumped around without rhyme or reason.

"I did." Riley decided it was her job to occasionally toss in a few words of agreement. Otherwise, she let Claire burn off steam.

"Touchdown!" Claire whirled in a circle, almost taking out two fans of the losing team.

"Watch it." The bigger man grumbled. "There's no need to rub our face in it."

"I wasn't." Claire tried to explain. "You see—"

"We don't care," shouted the man's companion.

"Come on," Riley grabbed Claire's arm when she would have continued the conversation. "Let's get out of here before you start a riot. Between the happy Knights' fans and the angry Chargers' fans, I don't want to be in the middle of it."

Riley steered Claire into one of the tunnels. Showing her ID to the guard, she bypassed the main exit.

"It will be awhile until Logan is finished changing. The press will be all over him for an interview." Riley unlocked the elevator using the passcode. "I assume you want to wait for him?"

"Absolutely."

"We'll wait where we can be comfortable." She pushed the button. As the elevator door shut, she laughed. "And someplace you won't cause trouble."

"I was excited."

"You were a menace." Riley grinned. "In the best sense of the word."

"CONGRATULATIONS. THAT WAS a great way to start the season."

Tired, but still jazzed from the game, Sean couldn't think of a better way to end his day than having a beautiful woman waiting for him. *If* that woman was Riley.

"We did okay."

"Hey, Riley." Sol Fellows called out. He had his arm around his wife and they didn't stop walking. "Did you watch me singlehandedly win the game? Whatever that pretty boy tells you, defense rules."

"You're a stud, Sol."

"Did you hear that, sweetheart? I've been telling you that for years."

"Thanks a lot, Riley." Racine Fellows yelled. "There will be no living with him now."

"Sorry."

Transferring his bag to his other shoulder, Sean held out his hand. Without hesitation, Riley took it.

"It's good to have family, isn't it?" he said.

For the first twelve years of her life, Riley had her grandfather. He had been her center. When he died, she would have been rudderless. However, Douglas Preston left her this. The Knights. A family.

Unconventional, but so what? They teased and fought and made up. Most importantly, they had each other's backs. If that wasn't a family, Riley didn't know what was.

"Did you drive?"

"Nope. I was hoping to get a ride with a sexy football player."

"Anyone I know?"

Riley stopped, her arms going around Sean's waist. He had on jeans and a sports jacket. The tie that he wore for televised post-game interviews hung out of his pocket.

"Maybe." She ran a finger over one of the dimples that always came out when he smiled. "I like you, Sean."

"You sound surprised." Sean turned his head, kissing her hand.

"A little." Riley sighed when he took the finger between his teeth, nibbling—ever so lightly. "I've felt a lot of things for you. I suddenly realized *like* wasn't one of them. Until now."

"We've had an unconventional..." Sean frowned. "What? Relationship? That word doesn't quite fit."

"I'm not sure there *is* a word that fits." They resumed walking. "Why don't we stay away from labels? I like you."

"And I like you." Stopping beside his silver Porsche. Sean opened the passenger door. He gave Riley a slow, lingering kiss before helping her in. "Buckle up."

Feeling warm inside, from the kiss, and Sean's words, Riley sat back, happy to be quiet while Sean drove. Expecting him to take the freeway, Riley was surprised when they didn't take the on-ramp.

"We both live in that direction."

"I won the bet."

"True."

"Now I'm collecting. One date." He sent her a grin that made her heart turn over. "Hopefully, you'll want more?"

"That's a loaded question if I ever heard one." Dropping it, Riley looked out the window. "Where are we going?"

"There's a little place about a mile from the stadium where I eat after every home opener. Call it my after game ritual. It's low key and smells like heaven. Spicy Italian." Sean paused. "I always go there alone."

Until now. Riley refused to read too much into it.

"Why are you sharing it with me?"

"I want to be with you."

Simple and direct. Oh, yes. She very much liked this Sean. Very much.

"You're wearing a bra."

"How did we get from dinner to bras?"

Riley looked down. And how could Sean tell what she was wearing? She had on three layers. Lacy camisole, t-shirt, and jacket.

"Unless you're hiding your true identity, Clark Kent, I want to know when you acquired x-ray vision?"

"It was a guess." Sean stopped the car. "I like you without."

"What difference does it make? My breasts are none of your business."

Jogging around the car, Sean helped her out.

"They occupy a lot of my thinking time these days. As does the rest of you."

Tongue in cheek, Riley said with a straight face, "You spend time thinking?"

"Is that your poor attempt at a dumb jock joke?"

"I thought it was pretty good."

"Amateur."

Sean proceeded to tell one joke after another, all concerning the woefully low I.Q. of the athletes. They were terrible. However, Sean told them with such enthusiasm and vigor, Riley fell under his spell. Wiping away the tears, she couldn't remember the last time she laughed so hard or so much.

A sense of humor. Another major plus on the side of why loving Sean McBride was not the worse idea in history. The pro column was filling up fast. As for the cons. They met one as soon as they were seated.

"Long time no see, Sean."

The long, lean brunette moved her boney ass so that it almost slapped Riley in the face. Peering around, Riley waited for Sean's reaction.

"We don't exactly run in the same circles, Ava. By the way, this is Riley Preston. Our circles are very similar. Riley, Ava Stanhope."

Riley smiled. *Well said, Sean.*

Ava wasn't impressed. At least, not with Riley. One down the nose look and Ava dismissed her as inconsequential. Running her thumb over her fork, Riley gauged how much effort it would take to jam the tines into a butt that had no discernible flesh on it.

"I'm in town for the next month. Then I'm off to Paris for a shoot. The cover of Vogue."

"Congratulations." Riley decided since they had been introduced, she was allowed to participate.

"It's a big deal."

"Well, sure. Vogue. That's a wow moment."

"I agree." Ava seemed to warm toward Riley. Her smile almost made it to her eyes. "Some people are less impressed."

"Sean catches an oddly shaped ball for a living. What does he know about fashion?"

"Hey." Sean waved his wrinkled tie. "This is Ralph Laurell."

"That's *Lauren*. And I bought you that tie."

"Whoops. Sorry."

Riley didn't buy Sean's apology any more than she bought his mix up on the name. Ralph Laurell, indeed.

"Will you call?"

"No, Ava. I'm sorry."

The model's eyes grew cold. "Your loss."

"Why is she here?" Sean didn't watch Ava walk away. He didn't follow the sway of her hips or catch the last inviting look she sent him over her shoulder. And just like that, the negative became a positive. One more for the good column.

"She doesn't eat. Ever. Why does she torture herself when the closest she gets to a piece of spaghetti is when she holds the box during a commercial?"

"Beats me." Riley wasn't going to defend a profession that extols the virtues of eating disorders. To punctuate the point, she slathered butter on a crusty piece of bread and took a big bite. "I love to eat."

"Would it be too much if I said I would love to eat you?"

Riley blushed. An honest to goodness, full-on blush. Red cheeks and all. She hadn't thought she was capable.

"It was too much?" Sean's smile told her he didn't regret the remark.

"I wasn't expecting it."

"Tell me if it makes you uncomfortable. I seem to want to say all kinds of outrageous things to you. However, I can curb the urge. Probably."

Riley had never been a fan of sexual innuendo or suggestive come-ons. She found them uncomfortable and crude. Yet when Sean spoke to her that way, she was impossibly turned on. It seemed it wasn't the words—it was the speaker.

"I'm okay with it."

"You are the sweetest thing." Sean took her hand. "If we were alone, I would lick that butter off you, one finger at a time."

"If we were alone, I'd let you." Riley glanced around the restaurant. "It can't be easy."

"What's that?"

"Being you. A famous athlete in a town that worships football. Do you have any idea how many people have taken your picture since we got here?"

"I stopped paying attention to stuff like that a long time ago. If I didn't, I would never go out. Like Gaige says, these people are the reason we can make a living playing a game. It's up to us to be as gracious as possible."

"I love Gaige."

"Me too. He's the best friend a man could hope for."

"Or a woman."

Sean looked at her, his eyes unreadable.

"You and Gaige. Did you ever...? You know what? Forget I asked. It doesn't matter."

"Sure it does." Riley put down her bread, giving Sean her complete attention. "The answer is no. Gaige has always been a big brother. Nothing more."

"Good. I know." Sean stopped her. "I have no room to judge. If you and Gaige had—been together, it would have made what's happening with us awkward."

"But not insurmountable?"

"I can't think of anything that would be. Can you?"

"Maybe." Riley didn't want to think about it, but how could she not? Now that the subject had been broached, she needed to ask.

"Tell me."

"Did you sleep with my mother?"

"No. Jesus, Riley. Why would you think such a thing?"

The shocked expression on Sean's face told Riley everything she needed to know. She felt foolish for asking, still it felt good to get rid of any lingering doubt. She would have dropped it right there if Sean hadn't seemed truly confused.

"My mother has a habit of using the team as her personal playground."

"I wish I could deny that, Riley." Sympathetic, Sean squeezed her hand. Then the implication hit him. "I was never interested."

"She was."

"Maybe."

Thinking back, Sean tried to pinpoint a particular come on. Corrine Preston wasn't subtle. When she was interested, she let them know. The players laughed about it—who would be this year's boy toy?

Some thought it flattering. Some were embarrassed. Almost all said yes. A rite of passage as a member of the Knights. Reports were that the experience was interesting. If you liked an older woman with a mommy complex.

"She wanted a son."

"To have sex with?" The second the words were out of his mouth, Sean wanted to call them back. "I'm sorry. That was inappropriate. She is your mother."

A fact that Riley knew Corrine wanted to forget—and often did.

"Technically. Giving birth does not a mother make. Or something like that. I'm not shocked by her behavior. Though I don't need the details."

"I agree. I can't remember the last time I spoke with your mother. As for the other?" Sean shuddered.

"Point taken." Laughing, Riley made a production of wiping her brow. "What a relief."

"Deal breaker?"

"I'm glad I don't have to decide. I can't imagine knowingly taking my mother's…" Riley searched for the word.

"Sloppy seconds."

"God. That is a nasty term."

"Mmm. And accurate—unfortunately."

Riley swirled her hands over her head and around the table.

"What are you doing?" Sean asked. Whatever it was, it was adorable. And hilarious.

"Clearing the air." Satisfied, Riley leaned forward, her blue eyes sparkling. "The subject has been discussed. Resolved. And filed away. Permanently sealed."

"Never to be opened again."

"Amen."

Unable to resist, Sean gave Riley a slow, lingering kiss. He knew cameras were going off all over the restaurant, but he didn't care. Let them enjoy the moment. He certainly was.

"What are the odds I'll be spending the night with you?"

"Better and better." Riley licked her lips, wanting to savor the taste of Sean. "Are you going to push your advantage?"

Sean wanted to. *God*, did he want to.

It would be easy to convince himself not to wait. They were adults. Unattached. Free to have as much consensual sex as their hearts desired.

Hadn't Riley made a point of telling him she was experienced? To what degree, he neither knew or cared. This Riley was worlds apart from the one who left for Boston five years ago.

The important part was, when the time came for them to be together, he wouldn't be taking advantage. Riley knew what she wanted. So did he. He wanted Riley. Yet, somehow, Sean knew it was too soon.

"I'm going to take you home. Kiss you until we are both crazy for more."

"Sounds good." Riley smiled, her mouth watering at the thought. "Correction. It sounds great."

"Then, I'm going home."

Riley thought he was kidding—until she saw his expression. Dead serious.

"Why? So you can suffer? Or take care of yourself?"

"I've been doing a lot of that lately."

Riley hoped that meant what it sounded like. Celibate Sean? There hadn't been the usual string of sexual partners in and out of his life since... when? She was dying to ask. To her surprise, Sean supplied the answer without any prompting.

"It's been awhile."

"Okay."

"Aren't you going to ask how long?"

"No." And Riley was proud of her restraint. "I haven't exactly been burning up the sheets."

"How long?"

Riley could tell Sean was teasing. Adorably charming. Jaw-droppingly handsome. Irresistibly sexy. It was a good thing she had come to terms with her love for him. Fighting her feelings would have been impossible.

"Long enough."

"How often do you," Sean's voice lowered to a whisper, "take care of yourself? And please, tell me you think about me."

"Do you...?"

"You've become my imaginary shower buddy." Sean's eyes dropped to her mouth. "If I told you what we did, you really would have a reason to blush."

"So why are we waiting?" Riley took a drink of water, hoping to cool her hopping hormones. It didn't work. "Why should we think about each other when we can have the real thing?"

When she put it like that.

"Check!"

SEAN TOOK RILEY home, but he didn't stay.

Leaving the restaurant had taken forever. The fans who had kindly left them alone while they ate, swarmed them before they could get to the car. Riley could tell Sean was impatient, yet he signed every autograph request and posed for pictures—graciously. The little boy with a cast on his arm received special attention. Sean wrote down the family's email address and promised to send along some Knights swag.

It delayed their departure, but it cemented Sean as one of the truly nice guys in football.

The next interruption didn't stall the evening. It ended it.

Sean's phone rang just as they pulled to a stop in front of Riley's downtown condominium. It was a few blocks away from Sean's loft. A complete coincidence, she assured him. As far as he was concerned, a happy one.

"Damn." Sean looked at his phone. "I have to take this."

As Riley listened to the one-sided conversation, it became clear she wasn't going to be hosting a night of wild, unrestrained sex.

"Why did they leave you? I agree. Fuck them. Tell me where you are. I'll have the car service come and get you."

The Knights, like most professional teams, made car pick-up available to their players who weren't in any condition to drive. On occasion, someone made the mistake of not taking advantage of the service—and the next day a DUI arrest was plastered over every sports blog and website. If the player was famous enough, the story went national. It was a headache every team dreaded.

"No. Do not get in your car. I'll be there in twenty minutes. Thomas? Promise me you'll stay in the bar until I get there. Good. See you soon."

"Jerry Thomas?"

Sean nodded. "He and a few of the guys were celebrating."

"I hope they didn't drive."

"No. They were together. When Jerry started overindulging, they tried to get his keys. He wouldn't give them up."

"And left him there?" Riley wanted names. That was unacceptable behavior. What if he was in an accident? What if he hurt, or killed, someone? So many lives ruined because he was an idiot and his friends didn't have his back.

"Rookies. I know, that isn't an excuse. However, it is the reason. They were intimidated by an older, and larger, teammate. I'll ream them out tomorrow."

"Will you tell Coach Coleman?"

"This is their first offense. As long as no one is hurt, we keep it strictly between players."

"Good."

"I'm sorry about this."

"Me, too." Riley kissed Sean's cheek. "We'll get there. Helping a friend is more important. Drive safe. It's starting to rain and the roads might be slick."

Sean waited until Riley was safely in her building before he drove off. He would help Jerry. Then, when he was sober, Sean would punch his lights out.

"I HATE YOU."

"You didn't have to come."

"Yes, I did."

They were in the film room, getting ready to watch highlights from yesterday's game. Most of the guys were there, the others filtered in. They looked like your average team after a Sunday playing professional football. Bruised and battered warriors of the gridiron. Some limped. Others groaned on the way down to their seats.

The difference between the Knights and half of the rest of the NFL? They had won their game. It made dealing with Monday's aches and pains a hell of a lot easier.

"I really appreciate you coming to get me, Sean." Jerry Thomas downed his entire bottle of water. He felt as if his body was slowly dying of thirst.

"Take another." Sean tossed him another bottle. "Alcohol dehydrates. Especially in the quantity you consumed."

"Never again." Jerry popped five aspirin before chugging the liquid. "My girlfriend broke up with me—right after the game. I decided to drown my sorrows. Instead, I made an ass out of myself and alienated my teammates."

"The girlfriend part sucks. I'm sorry, man." Sean clapped Jerry on the shoulder. "As for your teammates, they're the ones at fault. Leaving you alone was not cool." And Sean planned on letting them know just that.

"My fault for tagging a couple of rookies as my drinking buddies. Everyone else was gone. They seemed on board. At first."

"Then you gave them that defensive lineman stare and scared the shit out of them."

"Ya. I guess I did. The memory is a bit fuzzy."

"You had enough sense left to call me. I would have preferred to send a car."

"Shit." Jerry rubbed his temples. "You left with Riley Preston. No wonder you hate me. Did I interrupt at a critical moment?"

"Riley Preston?" Rob Cotter hit the back of Sean's chair with his foot. "Nice."

Several players lifted their heads like bloodhounds getting the scent of fresh meat. Sean groaned. He wasn't trying to hide his relationship with Riley. There was no reason. However, he didn't want her name bandied around the locker room.

Jocks could be crude dudes. Usually, it was done in good humor, but once they started, it was hard to turn them off. Sean was going to make sure each and every man knew nasty talk involving Riley was not going to happen.

Gaige beat him to it.

"Easy, guys. Remember, a lot of us knew Riley when she was a kid."

"Come on, Gaige. This one is too good to pass up." From behind, Rob wrapped an arm around Sean's neck. "The boss' daughter. Play your cards right and you'll sail through your next contract negotiation."

Sean threw off Rob's none-too-gentle embrace.

"I can take the heat, Cotter. But leave Riley out of it." Sean turned, his eyes hard. "Understood?"

"You want to tangle with me, McBride? I'll smash that pretty face to a pulp. Then I'll show your girlfriend what a real man can do."

With a savage growl, Sean prepared to launch himself at the other man. Rob Cotter outweighed him by a hundred pounds, but Sean didn't care. He would have taken the guy down if Gaige and Jerry hadn't grabbed his arms.

"Fuck off, Rob." Gaige shot the defensive lineman a warning look. "That is not cool. Move."

"Where?" Rob tried to maintain his cocky attitude, but Gaige had a way of knocking a guy down to size. It didn't help that he was hanging on to his job by a thread. He had lost a step. He knew it and so did everyone else. He couldn't afford to alienate the team's most important—and best liked—player.

"Any place but here."

"McBride can't take a joke," Rob mumbled, jumping seats until he was four rows back.

"Jesus, Sean. I thought you were going to rip Rob a new one. My head can't take this." Jerry shuffled away.

"Is that how it's going to be?" Gaige took the seat next to Sean. "You'll have to grow a tougher hide if you plan on dating Riley."

"I don't care what anyone says about me. Riley is off limits."

"Remember. Today she's the owner's daughter. In a few years, she will be the owner. Idiots like Cotter are bound to make cracks."

"Hell."

Gaige laughed. "It hadn't occurred to you?"

Sean felt sick to his stomach. He had gone over what seemed like a million obstacles between him and Riley. Her owning the team hadn't been one of them.

"How much do you think she has?"

"Right now? A lot. In five years? A hell of a lot more."

"Billionaires own football teams."

Sean swallowed. *Billionaire.* Why did that word stick in his throat? He hung out with rich people all the time. His friends were millionaires. *He* was a millionaire—as unbelievable as that seemed.

He grew up in a loving, normal family. A father who worked a nine to five job and a mother who stayed home with the kids and took care of the house. They had breakfast every morning before school and sat down together every night for dinner. Money had always been tight. Sean worked odd jobs to pay for his football expenses. For a while, it seemed he outgrew his cleats every other month.

The first thing he did when he signed with the Knights was pay off the mortgage on his parents' house. His mother cried. His father's chest puffed out. Filled with pride. His son. The NFL star.

Sean worked his ass off to earn that money. He enjoyed his lifestyle and all the perks. However, being able to take care of his family was the real reward.

Riley never had to worry about money. She was born with it. The amazing thing was, she worked her ass off too. She could have coasted through life, flitting from party to party. Mansion to mansion. She went to college and studied—hard. She didn't buy her grades; she earned them. She ran a business she started from the ground floor. Yes, she had advantages. But when it came down to it, she put in the work. Her success came from her brains and her sweat.

"Snap out of it." Gaige jabbed him in the arm. "Coach is speaking."

Sean sat up, his attention turned to Harry Coleman and yesterday's game. However, as he watched the plays and listened to the coaches, one thing kept echoing in the back of his mind.

Riley was a fucking billionaire.

Chapter Ten

"YOU ARE A snob."

"No."

"Yes."

"Maybe." Sean handed Riley a glass of wine. "But in my defense, I'm a really hot snob."

"That's a defense?" Riley looked him up and down over the rim of her glass. Faded jeans, bare feet, and a halfway unbuttoned white shirt. Add tousled ink-black hair and a slight five o'clock shadow and she almost forgot what they were talking about. "I'll give you hot. The snob part is another matter."

"I'm dealing with it."

Sean joined her on the couch. The one that overlooked the city. The one that up until now, he had never wanted to share. Riley, with her bright blue eyes and beautiful smile, seemed to fit. Perfectly.

"There isn't anything to deal with. My money isn't going anywhere. If I play my cards right, the amount is only going to grow."

"That's a cheery thought." Sean pictured stacks and stacks of bills, multiplying by the moment. "I like money, Riley."

"Damn straight you do. Look at this place. You didn't buy it with peanuts, fella."

True. He bought it for an outrageous amount of cash—without blinking an eye—because he knew he had another outrageous amount in the bank. It was an amount that grew daily because of endorsement deals and a huge salary.

"What do you see?" Sean pushed up his hair, exposing his forehead.

Not sure of the game, Riley was happy to play along. She leaned close. "What am I looking for?"

"The word hypocrite in big, bold letters."

"Ah." Riley kissed the warm space, her lips curving. "No words. That means you're redeemable. Permanent marks only appear when you're a lost cause."

Taking her glass, Sean set it out of harm's way. Sliding onto his back, he positioned Riley on top—her mouth even with his.

"One more thing before we start a marathon make-out session."

"Yes?"

"I buy dinner."

"When?"

"All the time. It's my thing. Promise me."

That was it? If Sean hadn't looked so earnest, Riley would have laughed. As it was, she couldn't resist teasing him.

"My poor wanna-be chauvinist. You just don't have it in you."

"Riley." Sean swatted her on the butt.

Again, that was it? She didn't tell him how she enjoyed his love pat. Maybe another time.

"Promise."

"Good."

Impatient, Riley touched his lower lip with her tongue. In retaliation, Sean took a bite. Riley moaned. That little nip sent sparks shooting in every direction through her body. Centering between her legs.

"Are we about to have sex?"

"No." Sean slid his hands between them and unbuttoned her jeans. "But I'm going make you feel very, very good."

"I want to make you feel good, too." Obligingly, Riley shifted so Sean could push the denim down her hips. "I've dreamed of this for years."

"We'll get there." He kissed her slowly, his tongue teasing her lips. "This doesn't end tonight."

"Promise?"

"I'm not going anywhere, Riley. Are you?"

"No." Riley sighed when Sean bit the side of her neck. She didn't know why that felt so good. She didn't care—as long as he never stopped. "I'm home."

Riley didn't mean Seattle. She meant here. With Sean.

It was too soon to tell him. He wasn't ready—neither was she. However, she was ready for this. She wanted—needed—the connection. No one had ever made her want it so much. She had the feeling no one besides Sean ever would.

"Lift your arms."

Her shirt disappeared, tossed in a random direction.

"Were you thinking of me when you got dressed?" Sean kissed her shoulder, his hands caressing her bare back. "No bra. I'm a very happy man."

"I have some very pretty ones. Lace. Satin. Silk."

"Another time you can put one on." He licked the spot he had bitten, then whispered. "Just so I can take it off."

Riley gasped. She didn't know when his hand had slid from her butt. Wanting more, she pushed her hips toward his talented fingers.

"I think I hit a hot spot." Testing his theory, Sean parted her legs to give himself better access. He smiled when she sighed his name."Interesting. Do you like that?"

"At the moment? More than breathing."

Holding her gaze, Sean put his glistening finger into his mouth. "Mmm. I think I've found my new favorite dessert. Peaches and…" He licked again. "Cream."

"*Now*, I should blush." Riley wasn't embarrassed—she was turned on.

"Maybe you are. People blush other places than their faces."

With breathtaking ease, Sean reversed their positions. He removed the rest of her clothing before arranging her legs so that he was kneeling between. Riley was on the sofa. Sean was on the floor.

With a wicked smile, Sean lowered his gaze. "I can see pink. Is it you, or your blush? It's kind of dark in here. I think I need a flashlight to be certain."

When Sean tried to stand, Riley clamped her legs around his waist "No?"

Sean grabbed her wrists, trapping them in one hand. She had him, and he had her.

"You aren't shining a light down there like some kind of perverted miner."

"There's an image." Sean lifted her hands over her head, leaning forward until their faces were so close, Riley could see the little flecks of green in his eyes. "A kiss?"

"Yes," Riley nodded. "Please."

Sean's words teased. However, his mouth let her know that she wasn't on this rollercoaster ride alone. Deep and passionate, his kiss was desperate. Intense. Like a narcotic. Somehow addictive and good for her at the same time.

"I need to touch you." Riley tugged at Sean's hold. "Let go, Sean. *And take off your shirt.*"

"Bossy." Sean ripped at the material, sending buttons flying in every direction. "Happy?" he asked.

"You have no idea."

It was one of those rare moments when fantasy became reality—and it turned out better than their wildest dreams.

Sean was a sculpted God. Defined muscles covered with smooth, lightly tanned skin. No one looked like that. Not without a lot of photoshopping. Yet, here he was. Riley would have spoken, but she was afraid if she opened her mouth, drool would run down her chin.

Afraid the image would disappear, Riley slowly reached out. Years of wanting. So sure this would never happen. She had been at this point before, only to wake. Frustrated and alone.

"You're real." Riley smiled slowly, her hand flat against Sean's warm, hard chest.

"One hundred percent. All natural. No fillers or preservatives."

"And I say Hallelujah. Praise genes, a weight room, and good nutrition."

Sean breathed deeply, his head falling back. Riley's touch was light—almost reverential. He wanted to give her all the time she wanted. He wanted to yell, *harder. Lower.* He kept his thoughts to himself because tonight was about her.

Riley's needs came first. Even if it killed him.

"Are you in pain?" Riley asked.

"I'm good," Sean said through gritted teeth.

"Good. Because I could do this all night."

Riley was teasing. She knew Sean was holding back—letting her play a little before the real fun began. She smiled, with wide innocence, when his eyes opened. Counting down from ten, Riley wondered how long it would take him to realize what she was doing. Ten. Nine. Eight. She didn't reach seven.

"You little witch." Sean pushed her back against the sofa. His body, so much bigger and stronger, covered hers.

"Did I do something wrong?" Riley batted her eyes.

"Teasing is great." Sean moved until he was even with one plump, hard tipped breast. "Until you have to pay the piper."

Riley watched—fascinated—as Sean's large hand covered her breast. The contrast was startling. And exciting.

His tanned skin was so much darker than the milky smoothness of her own. Hard and strong held soft and vulnerable. Riley trusted him to please her—never hurt or abuse.

"Didn't I tell you?" Sean's eyes met Riley's. "A perfect fit."

Before she could agree, Sean took her nipple between his teeth, biting until Riley swore she could see stars. Incandescent, blinding stars.

"Do you like that?" Sean licked, then bit again.

"Don't stop?" It was a question. Any second now, Riley would be begging.

"And kill us both? Never."

Lavishing equal attention to each breast, Sean feasted. He wrapped Riley in a velvet rope of desire. Tighter. Tighter. Until her breathing was labored and a fine sheen of perspiration covered her body.

"So responsive." He kissed each tip. "And we're just getting started."

The next kiss landed in between her breasts. Then, a little lower. Lower.

Riley licked her lips. She knew Sean's destination. His body pushed her legs apart, those impossible abs rubbing against her hot, wet center. The anticipation was excruciating—and wonderful.

When Sean lifted her leg, resting her calf on his shoulder, Riley knew she would orgasm the moment his mouth touched her. Remembering to breathe, she watched his head lower until she felt a whisper of air on her heated flesh.

"Will you scream for me, Riley?"

"Probably." Riley couldn't believe they were taking the time to talk. She felt Sean's lips move. Was he smiling? Unbidden, a laugh tumbled from her. "Is sex supposed to be funny?"

"If you do it right, sex can be anything. Everything. Let me show you."

The next few minutes were beyond Riley's imagination. Sean's magic mouth. So this was what all the fuss was about. She liked sex. She appreciated when a man took the time to go down on her. However, never—*never*—had she wanted it to go on and on.

Riley came. Long. Hard. And—she screamed.

She clutched at Sean's hair. Before she could take a breath, he drove her toward another peak. This time, he added one finger, then two. She tipped her head back, closed her eyes, and enjoyed the ride.

"One more," he urged when she thought they were through. "Three is a nice number, don't you think?"

"I can't, Sean."

Riley felt limp. Her body satisfied. She was ready to curl up and float on the memory. However, Sean was intent on drawing out every ounce of pleasure her body could stand. He wanted her to shudder and shake.

Riley didn't think she had it in her. She was wrong.

"I like that last sound you made."

Sean joined Riley on the sofa, gently pulling her into his arms.

"Shh." Riley snuggled close. "I'm in orgasm overload. I expect to stay this way for the next week. Wake me before the next game."

"I'll be out of town. Remember?" Sean picked up her prone body and headed for the bedroom.

"Call me."

"I have a better idea."

"Impossible. I want to wallow."

"You can wallow. In the bathtub."

"Okay."

"The secret to a compliant Riley has been revealed." Keeping her in his arms, Sean turned on the taps, setting them to the perfect balance of hot—not scalding. "Multiple orgasms and you are putty in my hands."

"Putty my ass." Riley pinched his.

Sean pinched back. Though his contained less sting.

"Hey. Watch it." Smiling, Riley laid her head on his shoulder. "Play nice. I'm a girl."

"No. You're a woman." Sean carefully deposited her into the tub. "Top to bottom. One hundred percent."

"This is a very large tub, Sean." Riley slid below the water's surface. Stretched out full length, her toes didn't reach the end.

"I like space," Sean said when she came up for air.

"Orgies? You and? Let's see. One. Two. Three. Four women?"

"I said space, smartass. You are the second person to use this tub."

Riley was surprised. And foolishly pleased. Most of the time she was fine with Sean's colorful and varied sexual past. She was realistic. This thing between them, whatever it was, could be a brief sidestep from his wild ways. An enjoyable glitch that would be fixed with a quick reboot.

However, for now, Sean was hers. Discovering the bathtub hadn't been the site of water games played with a bevy of beauties gave her a warm feeling. False happiness? Perhaps. Riley wasn't going to spend her time worrying about what the future held.

Live in the here and *now, Riley.* It was her new mantra.

"Instead of watching me soak, you could take advantage of all this space."

"Join you?"

"If you're shy, I'll look away while you undress."

"I'm not shy." Sean unbuttoned his jeans.

Riley smiled in anticipation. "I didn't think so. Are you wearing *the* underwear?"

The sight of Sean in nothing but a pair of tight boxer briefs was burned into Riley's memory. For a year, every magazine she had opened seemed to contain a full page ad of the NFL's sexiest player. It wasn't just Riley's opinion. There had been a poll and Sean won hands down.

A very famous designer took advantage, hiring Sean to endorse a new line of men's underwear. Sales skyrocketed and Riley had a constant reminder of what she thought she would never have.

Getting an up close and personal private viewing was one more fantasy fulfilled.

Without answering, Sean dropped his jeans.

"They pay me very well to wear these babies." He snapped the elastic waistband. "Luckily for me, they are very comfortable."

And very sexy. Riley didn't spend a lot of time comparison shopping—men's underwear was a bit out of her purview—but she gave these a big thumb's up. Then again, the bulge Sean sported would make anything look good.

"Got a problem there, mister?"

"It's nothing new. I've had it before. Knock wood—no pun intended—I'll have it again." He began to slide the material over his hips, then paused. "This is only a preview. What you are about to see is strictly window dressing. For tonight, think of my dick as a shiny toy you can't play with until Christmas."

"It's September, Sean." Riley licked her lips. "That Christmas reference better be your attempt at a clever metaphor. I'm not waiting four months to have—" Naked Sean made her lose her train of thought. "Holy crap."

"See something you like?"

"That is one big ass, *adult* toy you're sporting, my friend."

"Hands off," Sean warned when she started to reach out. "Play by the rules or I'm taking my balls and going home."

"Didn't your parents teach you to share?"

"Yes. And I will. Eventually."

Riley sighed. "Earlier, you called me a woman. I wasn't one before."

Sean settled into the tub. Her expression was so earnest. Her blue eyes filled with emotion. Taking her foot, he placed in onto his chest, smoothing his hand over the instep.

"Are we going to talk about it? Now?"

"We never have. This seems like a good time."

"Stripped bare, so to speak." Sean gave her big toe a light kiss. "It was five years ago, Riley."

"Eight."

"Eight? You would have been…?"

"Seventeen."

"I had no idea."

Sean looked mystified. Truly surprised—much to Riley's relief. His pity had been hard to handle when she was twenty. Three more years of it, even though she hadn't known at the time, would be hard to swallow.

"I'm going to tell you a story about a girl who decided, with one look, that she was in love. It isn't terribly flattering, so please keep that in mind. She was young and possessed with a stubborn kind of tunnel vision only found in a determined seventeen-year-old."

To her surprise, it didn't take her long. She always thought of her former Sean obsession as epic and far reaching. In truth, the whole thing could be recapped in ten minutes. Less, if Sean hadn't asked a few questions along the way.

Riley wasn't sure how she felt. She hadn't padded or embellished the facts. Suddenly, something that had occupied her life for so long had been reduced to a few succinct paragraphs. If written out? Two or three pages.

Funny. It took saying it aloud to finally put it in perspective.

"Sad? Pathetic? Creepy? Please check one of the above." Riley tried to make light of it, but she was on pins and needles waiting for Sean's reaction.

"I pick D."

"Ah. A wildcard answer." Riley took a deep breath. "Go on. Hit me. I can take it."

"Flattering."

"No, Sean. Don't let me off that easy. I was obnoxious." Riley cringed thinking about it. "I was a crazy kid. Filled with the odd idea that you would love me because to me, it made sense. A smart man would have run in the opposite direction. Instead, you tried to be nice."

"By putting my foot in my mouth." Sean shook his head. "Why are you beating yourself up? Especially at this late date?"

"Why aren't we having sex?"

"You lost me." Sean soaped up a cloth, making it nice and sudsy. Slowly, he ran it along her calf. He wasn't washing so much as caressing. It felt nice.

"What you did earlier? I'm all for it. Cartwheels and lollipops all around."

"Thank you."

"Hold off on the self-congratulatory back-pats, buddy. I'm adding a major but to that sentence. I want sex. Full-on, sweaty, mind-blowing sex."

"Riley—"

"I want your big, shiny, mouth-watering dick inside of me. I've been very, very good. I deserve my treat. Now."

"I…" Sean didn't know what to say. Yes, he did. "I've slept with a lot of women, Riley."

"No shit, Sherlock."

"You think you know. The truth is, you have no idea how many. I'm reluctant to admit that I lost count a long time ago."

"STD?"

"No. I'm clean. I've always been extra careful. And I regularly get checked by my own doctor. That isn't something I would want to come out during my team physical."

"Then I don't care, Sean." One or one thousand. What difference did it make?

"For some reason, I do." Leaning to his right, Sean touched a button. Bubbles began swirling around them. Riley felt the cooling water begin to heat. "Don't get me wrong. I enjoyed every hedonistic moment. It isn't that I want to turn back the clock or alter the past. Instead, I want this—us—to be different."

Riley felt her breath catch.

"I like different."

"I think I do, too."

"I want you to know, Sean. You don't have to prove anything to me."

"I need to prove it to myself."

Before Riley could blink, Sean turned her so her back rested against him. His erection was still at full staff.

"Isn't that uncomfortable?"

"It's... different."

"If I move a little I could—"

Holding her still, Sean laughed. Riley thought it sounded a little strained. She stopped squirming. She didn't agree with Sean, but it was his thing. She would respect it—and try not to make it harder on him.

"Want to share the reason for that lovely laugh?"

"Have you ever noticed? When you have sex on the brain everything is a double entendre?"

"Words can be a minefield." Sean put his lips near her ear. "If you have a dirty mind."

"Please." She playfully rapped her fist on the side of his skull. "I'm only borderline dirty."

"Stick with me. I'll push you to the next level in no time."

"I'm good where I am, thank you very much." Riley pulled Sean's arms around her waist. This was nice. Warm, frothy water and a big, strong, sexy man to share it. If she weren't careful, she would fall asleep.

"I should go home."

"Or, you could stay the night," Sean whispered, his hand covering her breast.

It wasn't sexual. Though it felt very, very good. It was sweet. Dare she hope, loving? She was tired. For now, that kind of thinking had to stay buried. Riley was tempted to stay. However, Sean was right. Slower was better.

"Another time."

Sean didn't argue. He helped her from the tub, leaving her to dry off while he retrieved her clothing. When he returned, he was wearing the same jeans with a fresh white t-shirt. It was a good look on him. Then again, what wasn't?

"Are we good?" he asked, holding out her shirt.

"I'm not leaving because I'm angry." Riley pulled on her jeans. Topless, she slipped her arms around Sean's waist.

"You have the softest skin."

"*That's* why." Reluctantly, she eased far enough away to slip on her shirt. "You keep touching me. And making remarks about my skin or how I taste."

"Bad Sean."

"Laugh all you want." Gripping his arm for balance, Riley slid on her shoes. "You want to be a good boy. I want to rip your clothes off. Chances are, if I stay, I'll compromise your purity before morning."

Later, after he walked Riley home, Sean stared at his bedroom ceiling, a grin plastered on his face. Yes, his sexual frustration was higher than he could remember. And sure, it would be better if Riley was here—in his arms. But damn. That woman could make him laugh.

Sexual purity, indeed. Closing his eyes, Sean took a deep breath, his body relaxing. *Only Riley.* He drifted, sleep closing in, and smiled again. *Only Riley.*

Chapter Eleven

THE TWO WOMEN, one blond, the other brunette, drew plenty of attention. This was a sports bar. On most days, the clientele was ninety percent male. On Sundays, the women who ventured in usually came with their husbands or boyfriends.

The crowd was raucous and focused on the game. However, when the final whistle blew, things changed. Fast. Especially when the Knights won.

"Put your money away, ladies. There is a line ten deep of men wanting to buy your drinks."

"What do you think?" Claire asked Riley, her eyes filled with laughter. They were at the bar in the same seats they occupied throughout the game.

"I think you should tell the men thanks, but no thanks." Riley handed the bartender a twenty. "We want two more drafts. Period. Whatever's left, keep for yourself."

"Will do. But I warn you, these guys hate to take no for an answer. Give me a signal if anyone gets out of hand."

"Why do men think all women are looking for male companionship?"

"Ego and too much cheap beer?"

"Mmm. Maybe we should have watched the game at your place."

The Knights were in New York this week. It was the featured game on Sunday night. A five o'clock start in Seattle.

Claire called to see if she wanted to watch the game together and Riley suggested *The Extra Point.* The idea of sharing the experience with other fans seemed like a good idea. Until now.

"You want to leave?"

"No." Riley clinked glasses with Claire. "The Knights won. Again. Logan had another hundred-yard-plus game and Sean caught a touchdown pass. We are going to celebrate. If anybody gets touchy-feely, you throw your beer in their face while I kick them in the balls."

"And *that* is why I knew we would be friends."

"Here comes idiot number one," Riley warned.

"Hey, beautiful ladies." His beer breath washed over her face. He wasn't bad looking. However, the swaying and glazed eyes were a hard look to carry off. It made his attractive factor plummet—fast.

"One push. He'll land on his butt and be out of our hair," Claire murmured.

Riley agreed with the assessment. Unfortunately, because the place was packed, the drunk was likely to take out five or six innocent bystanders on his way down. Entertaining, yes. Also, potentially dangerous.

"It isn't worth it. Let's go."

"Hey, where ya goin'?" idiot boy protested as they walked past him. He reached for one, then the other, missing both.

"Sorry about Ed." A tall, thin man grabbed hold of his friend before he toppled over. "Can we buy you a drink as an apology?"

"No."

Riley and Claire exchanged chagrined looks. Some guys never quit. Nor did their buddies.

They were almost out the door without further incident when out of the corner of her eye, Riley saw a familiar looking woman. A brunette with gravity defying breasts. Sapphire, her father's *personal assistant,* didn't look happy. In fact, she appeared to be on the verge of tears. With a sigh, Riley stopped Claire.

"You go. I'll meet you at the coffee place across the street."

"I'm not leaving you alone," Claire said. When Riley started weaving through the crowd, Claire was right behind. "What are we doing?"

Riley shrugged. It was too loud to explain the unexplainable. She felt bad about how she had treated Sapphire. The woman had been doing her job. And she was sleeping with Gerald Preston. Hadn't she suffered enough? If Riley could help out, she would be doing her good deed for the next month.

"I told you, I want to go home."

Riley heard Sapphire's teary words over the din.

"And I told you I want to stay," the man at the table yelled. "Leave. I don't care."

"Fine."

Sapphire seemed to lose her nerve when faced with a sea of drunk men.

"Come on, we'll get you out of here."

Riley might not have been Sapphire's idea of a savior, but she seemed to understand it was the boss' daughter or no one. Putting the woman between her and Claire, they made their way out of the bar without incident.

All Riley could think when they reached fresh air was, *never again.*

"Men are pigs." Sapphire cried. Her mascara ran, giving her raccoon eyes.

"Okay." Riley guided her across the street and into the coffee shop.

"Why?" Sapphire flopped onto the first chair she came to.

"Why what?" Claire asked Riley.

"I have no idea. By the looks of her, I doubt she knows. I'll flip you for the right to sit with her. The winner gets the coffee."

"No way. She's your...?" Claire searched for the word. "Friend?"

"Not even close, but I get the point. Make it strong and black."

Sapphire's forehead rested on the table. "Your father dumped me for a younger woman with bigger breasts."

What was she supposed to say to that? Naturally her father dumped Sapphire. It was his M.O. It was all fun and games until he grew bored or met someone else. The two events usually coinciding.

But bigger breasts? Sapphire's were squished against the table. How much bigger could you get?

"I hate my breasts."

Claire arrived with three steaming cups of coffee. Placing one in front of Sapphire, she said with genuine sympathy, "I'm sorry to hear that."

"One week after we started seeing each other, Gerald offered to buy me implants."

"Offered?" Riley doubted Sapphire had been given a choice. Not if she wanted the relationship to continue.

"Insisted," Sapphire admitted. "I wanted to make him happy. My body is grotesque and I'm all alone." The last three words came out in huge, gulping sobs.

"I'm sorry, Sapphire." Awkwardly, Riley patted the woman's back, handing her a napkin to wipe her eyes. "For my father and for how I behaved the day we met. I took my frustration with him out on you. It was wrong."

"It doesn't matter. I've given up everything for that man. I had a nice, solid boyfriend. Gerald seemed so worldly and sophisticated." Sapphire loudly blew her nose. "Today, I'd give anything for nice and solid. Did you see that idiot I was with? I've been reduced to accepting dates with athletic supporter salesmen."

"Can you make a living doing that?" Claire wanted to know.

Riley wiped her mouth, trying to hide her smile. Damn, this kept teetering between tragedy and farce. After her heartfelt apology, it would be rude to laugh. No matter how tempting Sapphire made it.

"Has he fired you?"

"Not yet. But it's just a matter of time. He'll want his latest floozy close by. How do you think *I* got the job?"

It would have been bad form to point out that Sapphire had just called herself a floozy. Instead, Riley took out one of her business cards.

"Here's what we're going to do." Riley scribbled her private number on the back of the card before handing it to Sapphire. "Finish your coffee. Then we'll get you a cab. Tomorrow when you're able to think things through with a clear head, decide if you want to have the implants removed."

"I can't afford it." Sapphire looked like she had hit bottom.

"My father paid to have them put in, I'll pay to have them taken out."

"Really?"

"It seems fair. And don't worry about your job. Stay if you want. If need be, I'll help you find another one."

It was amazing what a glimmer of hope did for a person's state of mind. By the time they put Sapphire in a cab, she no longer looked as if her world were ending. She even managed a smile, waving as the car pulled away.

"That was kind," Claire said as they walked toward her parked car. "I can't imagine taking pity on my father's mistress."

"She's a victim. I've seen his women come and go. There are predators, and there are women like Sapphire, who delude themselves into believing that my father truly loves them and that they will be different from all the others. Trust me, they never are."

"The surgery." Claire hit the remote, the car's headlights engaging, signaling the doors were unlocked. "That was more than a friendly gesture."

"I'm giving her a choice." Riley slid into the passenger side, then closed the door.

"She chose to have those things put in, Riley. No one held her down."

"Love has a way of clouding your judgment."

Riley's experience hadn't been as extreme. However, at twenty-five, it was easy to say she would never let a man talk her into doing something that, deep down, she didn't want to do. Five years ago, she didn't know what she would, or wouldn't, have done if Sean had asked.

"I'm lucky to be in love with a man who likes me the way I am."

Riley looked Claire up and down. Tall, gorgeous, and smart as a whip. The woman was practically perfect. But a man—the wrong man—could always find something with which to tear down a woman.

Gerald Preston was the perfect example. Riley's advice? Run, ladies. Run hard and fast in the opposite direction. Unfortunately, her father had enough of the three Cs to pull woman after woman into his web.

Cash. Charm. Clout. A heady combination that often spelled disaster for someone like Sapphire.

"Think she'll make that call?"

"I hope so. But," Riley gave Claire a half-smile, "it's up to her."

TWELVE FIFTEEN. RILEY'S visitors, when she had them, rarely arrived after eight. She didn't mind staying out late. However, when she stayed in, anything after ten equaled the middle of the night.

The intercom buzzed again.

"Yes, Stuart?"

"He wants it to be a surprise, but I can't let anyone up without announcing them."

"Who? And damn straight you need to announce them."

"Mr. McBride." Stuart's voice vibrated with excitement. "*Sean* McBride," he qualified.

Riley grinned. He must have come straight from the airport. The team's plane had made good time. Not that it mattered. Anytime was fine with her. No hour was too late for Sean.

"Send him up, Stuart."

"Right away."

She didn't know who was more excited by Sean's arrival. Her or Stuart. Riley rushed to the bathroom, checking her image. She hadn't been asleep, only reading in bed. Still, she took the time to fluff her hair. Her mouth still felt minty fresh.

Lavender satin and lace. Not Riley's usual sleep garb. An impulse had her donning the nightgown. Or had it been a premonition?

The knock on her front door brought a wave of anticipation. It had only been three days, but it felt longer. She missed him. It was that simple. And it made her happy that after a long, exhausting roadtrip, the first thing he wanted was her.

"Hi."

Sean didn't look tired. He stood in the hall outside of her condo all sexy and masculine.

He sported a bit of stubble on his face and a smile that made her heart race. Jeans, a leather jacket, and lace-up sneakers that looked like a cross between hiking boots and high-tops. Riley knew each piece of his outfit sported a designer label. However, Sean wore them with a casual ease. He never looked like he was trying too hard to be cool.

As a result, he was the personification of the word.

An answering smile curved Sean's lips. Without a word, he entered her home, lifting her into his arms. Riley locked her legs around his waist, slammed the door, then burrowed her face into his clean, soft hair.

"I missed you."

"I'm glad," she whispered, breathing deep. Nothing but soap and Sean. It was a scent she wanted to drench herself in.

Sean pulled back until his eyes met hers. Hazel flecked with green and gold, glowing with need. His gaze dropped to her lips, his groan deep when her tongue moistened the surface. In an instant, he closed the gap that separated them.

The kiss bordered on desperate. It only took a second for it to cross over. Riley sank into the feel of Sean's mouth covering hers. He consumed her. Eagerly, she opened to his questing tongue, wanting more. Needing everything.

"Are we having a sleepover?" Riley asked when Sean headed down the hall.

"Sleep?" Sean tossed her on the bed. "Eventually."

Riley rested on her elbow, not wanting to miss the show. Off came his jacket followed by a white t-shirt. This view alone was worth any price of admission.

His skin was a light brown. As with his black hair, the tone was a testament to the Cherokee blood that ran on his mother's side. Smooth, with a slight dusting of hair that formed an interesting V above the waistband of his tight cotton briefs.

Riley wanted to touch, kiss, and taste very mouthwatering inch.

"I like the nightgown," Sean said, slowly lowering his zipper. "But it has to go."

Riley opened her mouth, ready to respond with a quick quip. Whatever she was about to say melted from her brain when Sean removed a condom from the pocket of his jeans.

"That looks serious." Riley swallowed, hoping she knew what the foil packet meant.

"I don't carry them around for show."

"Should I sing a chorus of Hallelujah?"

"I'll have you singing, Riley." Grinning, Sean kicked aside his shoes and jeans. "If you want to get a head start, be my guest."

"I think I'll save my energy."

She thought Sean taking his clothes off was a show? That was a pale imitation compared to a front row seat to the condom roll.

"What made you change your mind?"

"You want to go into that now?" Sean asked. He placed a knee on each side of her, causing the mattress to dip. "All the way to New York I called myself a hundred different kinds of fool for leaving us both wanting. All the way home, I thought of nothing but this. I want you, Riley. I hope that says it all."

"It does."

"Good." Sean raised the hem of her nightgown. "So pretty."

"Lavender," Riley breathed. "Silk and lace."

"I wasn't talking about lace." He ran his hand up the inside of her thigh, stopping where his gaze was focused. "But you do feel like silk."

No more talk. No more questions. Riley concentrated on Sean. On his touch and the way only he could make her feel.

"I want to be inside of you. Ready?"

Riley was ready. She had been for years.

"Yes. Now, Sean. Please."

"Since you asked so nicely." Sean nudged at her, finding a warm, welcoming wetness that left little doubt how ready she was. "And since I can't wait a second longer. Feel me, Riley. Every bit of me is for you. Only you."

Only her. Sean was talking about sex. Here. Now. Riley understood that. However, it was impossible not let her heart open a bit more. With wanting and hope.

The ride was wild. Sean took her up. Higher and higher. Then pushed her over. Falling with her. There wasn't a crash. Riley floated back to Earth.

The first thing she became aware of was Sean's ragged breathing. The weight of his body on hers comforted instead of crushed. He was big and strong, outweighing her by a hundred pounds, but Riley didn't care. She wanted to stay like this, hot, sweaty and oh, so satisfied, as long as possible.

"I should move."

"No." Riley tightened her grip on his waist.

"I should say thank you."

She smiled, her lips brushing his shoulder.

"Okay."

Chuckling, Sean shifted until he was on his side with Riley draped over his chest. Somehow—experience, she supposed—he removed the condom and pulled the covers over with little effort.

"Thank you, Riley."

Riley smiled again, this time with her mouth against his. After a lingering kiss, she relaxed against him.

"If you are very, very good, I'll let you thank me again. All night long."

Chapter Twelve

THE KNIGHTS' FIRST loss of the season occurred three days after the picture of Riley and Gaige burned up the internet.

No one thought there was a connection. The official team statement said as much. The fact that they addressed the issue spoke volumes. Everyone could deny it all they wanted. The average Knights' fan believed there was a rift in the locker room.

Normally, it was a simple matter to gloss over a minor argument. These things happened all the time in the course of a season. However, when the perceived problem was a love triangle between Gaige Benson, Sean McBride, and Riley Preston, no amount of sugar coating worked.

The press smelled high-priced blood, and they weren't letting go of the scent.

"It's ridiculous."

"I agree."

"I've hugged Gaige hundreds of times."

"I've seen you do it."

"Why now?"

"We all know the answer to that."

Riley and Sean were having dinner with Logan and Claire at the newly engaged couple's downtown apartment. It was a rental. Logan hadn't wanted to buy until he knew his comeback was a success. He was making a base salary laden with incentives.

By the looks of things, Logan Price was going to have a hefty bank account by the end of the season. He and Claire planned on looking for someplace permanent in the spring.

"A hug is a hug. Until it becomes common knowledge that you're dating a member of the team—and the man you were caught hugging is a different Knight."

"And not just any Knight. Gaige Benson. Maybe the most famous football player in the country. *And* Sean's best friend."

Claire summarized the situation perfectly. Said aloud, it sounded crazier than ever.

"What does the team think?"

"Riley." Sean rubbed her back. "They know Gaige. Half of the guys have been with the team long enough to remember you. We told them there is nothing to the story, and they believe us."

"He's right." Logan joined them in the living room. He handed them each a cup of coffee. "The offensive line offered to kick some blogger butt if they keep pecking at you."

Riley smiled. Logan's personal drama happened while she was in Boston. His injury during his rookie season and failed return the next year. She was glad to be here to witness his improbable comeback. The triumph over adversity angle made his story irresistible. Happily, the man was a nice guy.

His love for Claire was obvious to the most casual observer. Riley approved. For the team. And for her friend.

"It's a tempting offer, Logan. Unfortunately, there's no taking it back. Any picture can look bad with the right spin."

Riley knew when the picture was taken. The day she visited Coach Coleman during practice. Gaige and Sean joined her on the sidelines. The photographer caught the moment she hugged Gaige. Innocent enough. Until you added the caption. *Owner's daughter. Spreading the love around?* It went on to mention Riley and Sean's relationship.

Riley knew as gossip went, it could have been worse. Then the

Knights lost. Gaige threw an interception. Sean dropped a pass. And suddenly, the world was ending.

Riley was cast in the role of Pandora, Delilah, and Yoko Ono. All rolled into one. *One game!* If they lost again on Sunday, she wouldn't be able to show her face in public.

Sean put a more positive spin on it.

"When we win on Sunday, all of this shit will be forgotten."

"From your mouth to the football God's ear."

THE KNIGHTS WON. Big.

A home game, the stadium was packed to the rafters. Because the game was against a bitter division rival, the crowd was particularly vocal. Unlike the last time, Riley didn't sit in the crowd. The owners' box wasn't the perfect solution, but she refused to stay at home. She hadn't done anything wrong. Hiding away as though she had, wasn't the solution.

"I'm surprised to see you. I can't fault your nerve."

Riley glanced at her mother. Overdressed, as usual. In Corrine Preston's opinion, diamonds and fur worked for any occasion.

"I always support the team."

"Is that what they're calling it these days?" Corrine's laugh had a sharp edge to it. "In my day—"

"In your day? You have the nerve to pull out that chestnut?" Riley was in no mood to turn the other cheek. Her mother was likely to slap it. "I know how many Knights I've slept with. Want to compare lists?"

"You smug little bitch."

"Why are *you* here, Mother? You only show up when there's a new crop of rookies to prey upon."

Riley regretted the words the moment she said them. Not out of respect. That ship hadn't sailed—it never left port. Exchanging barbs with Corrine served no purpose. When she was younger, it gave her a sick little thrill to mentally out joust her. Now, it made her tired.

"You believe you have it all, don't you? Money, youth, power. It's an illusion. Nothing is forever. In twenty years, that pretty football player you're screwing will be on his third, much younger wife. And you'll have what? This team? You won't be so sassy then."

Corrine glided away, leaving behind a cloud of French perfume and bitterness. Unlike her mother, Riley knew her life would never be an empty round of boring parties and charity luncheons.

Life was a series of choices. Some good. Some bad. Corrine chose to marry Gerald Preston. She chose to stay married to him. If her mother were unhappy, she had only herself to blame.

"I see your mother is doing her best to spread sunshine all over the place." Ross Morrisey offered Riley a sandwich. The gourmet grilled cheese sat untouched on his plate beside a scoop of equally fancy potato salad.

"No, thanks."

Ross took a sip of scotch. Riley knew the bar was stocked with each board member's favorite drink. Ross liked an aged single malt.

"She almost had my wife in tears. I've never hit a woman, but—"

"This is where I should step up as the loyal daughter." Reconsidering, Riley took the sandwich. "I've never defended her before, I can't start now."

"No one blames you, Riley. Your parents are, for the most part, indefensible snakes."

It was said with no heat or rancor. She wondered how two people could be so coldly disliked. Didn't heat automatically accompany hate? Or was it hate? Riley disliked her parents. She didn't care enough to hate them.

"You knew my grandfather. How did such a wonderful man produce a son like Gerald Preston?" Riley and Ross had spoken on many subjects. This was one they had avoided. Today, for some reason, Riley needed an answer.

"Douglas was a good man, Riley. However, he wasn't perfect. It's good and right that you idolize him. I think if he were here, he would be the first to admit he wasn't the best father in the world."

"But—" Riley started to protest.

"Don't get me wrong. Douglas wasn't abusive. He was neglectful.

You had the best of him—after he made his money and wasn't driven by ambition. Gerald didn't see very much of his father. It isn't an excuse for how he is now. It is the reason, at least partially, that he resents you."

"Resents?"

"Too mild?" Ross' words had a teasing tone.

"I don't know. I guess it's as good a word as any. What my parents feel for me has always been a mystery. I'm sorry my father didn't grow up knowing the Douglas Preston I knew. I wonder if it would have made a difference."

"You blow me away, Riley." Ross shook his head. "You have insight the rest of us can only dream about."

"Insight? Is that what it is? I thought I was stating the obvious. My father is a petty, small-minded man. He has no reason to be. He was given every advantage. Education. Money. He's seen the world. Read extensively. Yet for some reason, his view is narrow and self-involved. Do you think that's because of his daddy issues? I don't. I think it's all on him."

"Run for president. You'll have my vote. Laugh if you will, I'm serious."

"I know. *That's* why I'm laughing. I thought you were my friend. Why would you wish something like that on me? Besides, I'm a Democrat. And a woman."

"Shh." Ross looked around in mock horror. "You're standing in a room of ultra-Republicans. You just spoke a dirty word."

"Democrat?" With her tongue only half in her cheek, Riley added, "or woman?"

Ross' bark of laughter garnered a lot of attention. Wanting to know the source of the joke, Riley soon found herself surrounded by half of the Knights' board of directors. These were men she worked with in her consulting business. Getting an in with them had been simple. Once Ross was in, the rest followed.

Riley had used one of her grandfather's business tactics. When trying to infiltrate a group, go for the alpha first. It worked. The bonus was, Riley had acquired a friend as well as a client.

Ross Morrisey was one of the good ones and Riley was glad to have him on her side.

Halftime rolled around and the Knights were well in control of the game. They coasted through the second half, Coach Coleman taking out most of the starters in the fourth quarter.

So much for her womanly wiles destroying the team.

Riley let herself into her condo. She and Sean had agreed that it didn't make sense for her to wait around after the game. His routine varied depending on how may news outlets requested interviews. He planned on joining some of the guys for a drink.

Riley told Sean to go home and get some sleep when he was finished. They didn't need to see each other every day. Sean didn't agree. He would call when he was on his way. No later than eight o'clock.

She checked her messages. There wasn't anything that needed her immediate attention. Riley opened her refrigerator. One look told her what she already knew. Dinner would either be cereal and milk that had an iffy sell-by date—or takeout.

Every now and then. Check that. More often than not, when she found herself in this situation, Riley considered learning how to cook. Something beyond toast and scrambled eggs. Occasionally, she worked herself into the belief that she would take a class.

World Cuisine 101. Travel the globe from the comfort of your own kitchen.

The urge lasted until Riley remembered why she didn't cook. She didn't want to. To be good at something, and Riley would insist on being great, she had to want to do it. Preparing an amazing meal was something to be admired, but she didn't aspire to that talent.

Seattle was home to some amazing restaurants. Riley grabbed her phone. It would be a shame not to take advantage of them.

Before she could decide what she was in the mood for, her phone rang. It was Claire.

"I'm on my way. I know it looks bad, but try not to overreact."

"What are you talking about?"

"Well, crap. Never mind. I'm just entering your building. I'll tell you when I see you."

"Claire—"

"Never mind announcing me," Claire said. "She's right here. Riley, tell him I can come up."

Riley pictured Claire holding out her phone. "It's all right, Stuart."

"Okay, Ms. Preston."

"Why don't you meet me at the elevator?"

"What?" Riley couldn't figure out what was going on. "Why? Are you carrying something large and cumbersome? If so, Stuart would be happy to help."

"No. I just… You know what? Never mind. I'm already on your floor."

There was a knock. Knowing who was there didn't stop Riley from automatically checking the peephole.

"What is going on?" she asked as she let Claire in.

Claire dropped her purse on the sofa.

"There isn't a pretty way of doing this. Here."

Puzzled, Riley took Claire's phone. What she saw cleared up the mystery. And made her blood boil.

"You have to be fucking kidding me."

It was a picture of her and Logan. Laughing. Riley had her hand on his arms and she was leaning in. It could be construed as intimate. Or a sane, rational person could see it for what it was. Two friends sharing a moment. Period.

The blogger, or whatever the person who posted the picture called himself, was not sane or rational. Under the photo, it read: *At it again? Not happy with two Knights, Riley Preston wants the entire team. Whether they are married or not.*

"The entire team? Three men are the entire team?" Riley couldn't take it in. Then she realized the implications. "Claire. I'm sorry. This is a slap at you, too."

"Indirectly." Claire waved off Riley's concern. "Someone is going after you. You're being painted as an aggressive man vacuum."

"That's lovely." Riley looked at the photo again. "I suppose it could be worse."

"It is."

"I don't want to know, do I?"

"If I could spare you, I would." Claire's eyes were filled with sympathy. Scroll down."

Resigned, and sporting a major knot in her stomach, Riley moved her thumb over the screen. There were five more pictures. With five different players. The content was similar to the others. Friendly smiles and casual touches.

Three of the players pictured were married, the other two in long-term, committed relationships.

Each caption was nastier than the last. Finally, under a photo montage, were two words. *Team Bicycle?*

"As in everybody's had a ride?"

The phone belonged to Claire. Otherwise, it would be across the room, smashed against the wall. To be safe, Riley handed it back.

"I don't give a flying leap what anyone thinks of me." Riley didn't simply say it. She meant it. "The first picture was one thing. I'm worried about the players' wives. If things are uncomfortable at home, it could translate to the locker room. Then to the field."

"Nip it in the bud."

"How?"

Riley was frozen. Inside and out. Sensing her friend's emotions, Claire gently led her to the sofa. Once she had her seated, she went to the kitchen.

"Be proactive," Claire said as she filled the kettle.

Riley owned few appliances. She didn't use them, why have them sitting around gathering dust? However, an electric kettle was a must. Coffee was her drink of choice. She spread the love to coffee shops all over the city. At home, she went for tea. In her opinion, making a good cup of coffee was an art that she left to the experts. Tea, on the other hand, required only hot water and a bag. Even she couldn't screw that up.

"My grandfather was my first love. Football my second." Closing her eyes, Riley rubbed her temples. A headache was imminent and it was going to be a doozy. "I lost him. Am I going to lose my team, too?"

"No." Claire didn't hesitate. "Absolutely not. The players have your back, Riley. Most of the wives don't know you. Call them. Arrange a meeting."

"A meeting." Riley ran the idea around in her head. It made sense. "This could be tricky. Casual girlfriends shouldn't be included, but how can I determine the state of a relationship?"

"Or," Claire set a steaming cup of tea on the glass table in front of Claire. "You go to the leaders. Every group has them. The Knights have Gaige and a few other guys, and wives have…?"

"Racine Fellows."

Claire's solution was brilliant. Single out the alpha. It worked in business. Why not in a sticky situation not of her making?

"Sol's wife." Claire smiled. "I like her. She shoots straight."

Claire characterized Racine Fellows to perfection. She and Sol married straight out of high school. While he played college ball, Racine had a baby, held down a job, and went to school. By the time Sol was drafted by the Knights, Racine had her degree and two small children.

Most women would have relaxed and enjoyed her husband's success. Not Racine. She started her own business and gave birth to twins. She was a good mother. A loving wife. A kick-ass CEO. And one of Riley's all time favorite people.

Riley decided to wait until the next day to contact Racine. Sunday nights were sure to be busy. Four kids who had school the next day and a husband back from his weekly game. Riley didn't want to be any more of a disruption. Especially when she needed a favor.

"Tomorrow is soon enough—" Riley picked up her phone. Looking at the caller ID, she smiled. "Hello, Racine. We were just talking about you."

Ten minutes later, Riley felt as though everything was going to be okay.

"You did a lot of nodding and not much talking. I take it from your expression Racine has things under control."

"She's a wonder. And maybe a mind reader. We are going to lunch at her home tomorrow."

"We?"

"She's invited a few of her close friends. Plus the wives and girlfriends of the men in the pictures. The only way to fight stupidity is with intelligence. That's a direct quote from Racine."

"I think I'm in love."

"Stand in line." Riley took a sip of tea. It was cold, but she didn't notice. "I don't know if this is about the team or me."

"Both?"

"Maybe. Racine is helping us divert potential disaster because her husband's team is involved. And because she's a friend." Riley looked at Claire. "I seem to be blessed in that department."

"Why do you think that is?"

"Beats me."

"You only have good friends if you're willing to be one. I think I can speak for Racine when I say we're lucky to have you."

"I'm about to get weepy. I think we need something stronger than tea."

"Amen."

As Riley opened the cabinet where she kept the liquor, the intercom buzzed.

"Stuart, if they aren't carrying a box with pizza in it, we are not home."

"No pizza. Will egg rolls and fried rice do?"

Riley smiled. Pizza be damned. Chinese and Sean? Yes, please.

"I should go."

"Is that Claire?" Sean asked. "Tell her to stay put. Logan and Gaige are right behind me."

"Come on up. We're about to break out a very old bottle of whiskey."

"Are we celebrating?"

Riley heard the concern in Sean's voice. He must have seen the pictures. Take-out and friends. He was surrounding her with plenty of support. If Riley hadn't loved him before, her heart would be making a fast tumble.

"Bring me an egg roll and I'll tell you about it."

"You have a deal."

THERE WAS NO doubt in Riley's mind that women ruled the world. At least her world.

Lunch at Racine Fellow's house wasn't like the get-togethers Riley had witnessed growing up. There were no crustless sandwiches accompanied by tiny bowls of clear, tasteless consumé.

Racine served stick to your ribs fare, and she expected everyone to eat like they meant it. No picking at your food or worrying about calories. What was the point of living if you spent ninety percent of your time hungry and miserable?

"Try some of those sweet potatoes." Riley noticed when Racine coaxed, her Georgia accent became thicker.

"My trainer would have a fit if she saw all this food." Diane Porter sighed, then took another bite of fried chicken. The girlfriend of tight end Jamal Fisk was an internationally known model with her own reality show. "Oh, who the hell cares. I pay her, not the other way around."

"There you go." Racine clinked wine glasses with the other woman.

Riley appreciated the casual atmosphere. Jeans, sneakers, flats, ponytails, and minimal makeup ruled the day. Ten women with little in common except football. Or rather, the men who played the game.

They were members of an exclusive club. Thousands applied, few were accepted. And each was determined to hold on to what they had. It made Riley's position awkward.

Girlfriend? She was reluctant to categorize her relationship with Sean. It was too new and precarious. Right now, she enjoyed all things Sean. His company. His sense of humor. His fabulous athletic body and the unbelievable way his slightest touch made her feel.

They hadn't discussed what they were to each other or anything about the future. Riley wanted more. She wanted it all. However, she knew it could change on a dime. She enjoyed the here and now. As her grandfather used to say, *worry about today. Tomorrow has a way of taking care of itself.*

As with all of Douglas Preston's advice, Riley took it to heart. Today wasn't about Sean. It was about convincing a group of women who didn't know her or trust her. Every day they dealt with groupies trying to seduce their men. The pictures had to have stirred up some fierce emotions."

"How are you doing?"

"No one has spit in my eye. Yet." Riley smiled at Racine. "I've been mingling. When I join them, the temperature cools considerably."

"You have three things going against you."

"Only three?" Riley maintained her smile, but inwardly, she groaned.

"First. They don't know you. Not your fault. Today is the first step in remedying that," Racine assured her. "Second. You are management, which gives better access than your average groupie."

"Groupie? Me?"

"Three," Racine pushed on. "Your mother."

Riley swallowed. Hard. She had thought of that but hoped it wouldn't be an issue. Hearing it from Racine shot that hope all to hell.

"I wish I didn't have to ask this. How many of their men has my mother…?"

"Hit on?"

"I'll breathe a sigh of relief if that was as far as she got."

"Nine women. Nine hits. No completions. That I know of. People lie. I doubt that comes as any surprise."

Riley sighed. Well, crap. "Sol, too?"

"During his first training camp."

Riley wished the floor would open up and swallow her alive.

"Racine. I don't know what to say."

"Sol turned her down. Flat." Racine's eyes grew hard when she thought about it. "But, even if he hadn't, it wouldn't be your fault, Riley."

"We wouldn't have become friends."

"No. We wouldn't have had the chance. I would have killed Sol. Then your mother. Right now, I would be serving a life sentence over in Walla Walla."

135

"Is that the secret to a long marriage? The threat of death?"

"That and a whole lot of love."

Riley felt a twinge of envy. Hell, more like a hard twist—right around her heart. Love wasn't easy to find—or hold on to. Riley searched her memory for another couple she knew who had what Racine and Sol had. Claire and Logan. They were solid to the core.

That made two. Hardly encouraging numbers.

"Come on. They are full of food and good wine. Time to make our move."

Riley followed Racine. She wasn't going to stand in the corner like a naughty child. Shoulders back. Chin high. On the outside, she looked strong and confident. No one needed to know that her insides felt like melting Jell-O.

"Would everyone gather round? Don't be shy. There are plenty of seats."

Slowly, the women joined Racine and Riley in the spacious living room. A large moss green sectional filled the space in front of a floor to ceiling stone fireplace. Chairs in a lighter complimentary color were scattered around. It was inviting and homey, with a touch of sophistication. Just like Racine.

Racine didn't waste time. Once everyone was seated, she addressed the elephant in the room with her usual candor.

"We've seen the pictures. I know without a second's hesitation that they are completely innocent and as bogus as a three-dollar bill. Your men have said as much. Am I right?"

"Where there's smoke, Racine," Lynette Trenton said, crossing her arms.

It was a hostile gesture that told Riley the woman had already made up her mind. It didn't help that Lynette's husband Kyle was known for his roving eye. The defensive lineman had a reputation for fooling around on the road—and in Seattle.

"There is no smoke, Lynette. Take away the captions and none of us would look twice at the pictures."

"I believe Miller when he says there's nothing to it." Piper Billings' voice wasn't loud but it was firm. Her husband was a rookie out of BYU, who made the team as a punt returner. She was sweet and shy. Grateful, Riley knew it must have been difficult for the young woman to speak up.

"Piper, you would believe your husband if he said the sky was green."

"Oh, button it, Lynette." Jeanie Skaggs squeezed Piper's hand. Jeanie wasn't there as a wronged wife. She, like Racine, was a respected football wife. "Most of us came here today because we felt it was a good idea to clear the air. You and Felicity are the only ones who think anything is going on. The rest of us trust our husbands."

"I trust Neil," Felicity Crandall insisted.

"I heard what you were saying, Felicity. You parroted Lynette's sentiments word for word," Jeanie sneered.

"I'm a supportive friend."

"You're a doormat with big size ten footprints on your back."

"I do not wear a size ten," Lynette protested. Unsuccessfully, she tried to tuck her feet under the sofa.

"Ladies." To Riley, Racine whispered, "And I use the term loosely."

Riley bit back a smile.

"Bickering isn't getting us anywhere."

"What about her mother?" Lynette threw that out with a smug smile.

"What about her?"

"Please, Racine. The term like mother, like daughter comes to mind."

"It has nothing to do—"

"May I say something?"

"Please," Racine said. "Riley didn't have to come here. So please. Hear her out."

"Racine has known me for ten years. Claire and I are new friends, but it feels like I've known her my whole life."

"Good for you." Lynette didn't sneer her words, but it was a near thing. "Is this where we get the poor little rich girl routine?"

"Hell, no." Riley stood up straighter. "My grandfather was Douglas Preston. He was the finest man I have ever known. I live my life by the example he set. Sometimes I fall short. But understand this. I am proud of who he was and the legacy he left me. Poor little rich girl? Grandpa would laugh his ass off over that term. And kick mine if he thought for a second that was how I portrayed myself."

The trepidation that had plagued her had vanished in the face of Lynette's ill-disguised contempt. She wanted the support of the women, but she wasn't apologizing to anyone for who she was.

"You tell her, Riley," Jeanie called out.

"It comes down to this." Riley purposefully looked each woman in the eye. "Football—the Knights—is what gives all of you the lifestyle you rightfully enjoy. Someone is trying to screw with that."

"Don't say it, Lynette," Racine warned.

Screwed. Not the best choice of words. Riley laughed.

"I tried to be delicate and look where it got me," Riley laughed. "Someone is fucking with the Knights and I refuse to let them. I love this team. I hope you feel the same."

"I do," Piper declared. Riley's curse word had turned her cheeks pink, but her voice was strong. "The Knights took a chance on Mark when no other team wanted him. I'm with you, Riley."

The other women called out their support, even Felicity Crandall. Lynette didn't want the issue to die that easily.

"What is this, a Girl Scout Jamboree? Where's the campfire so we can join hands and sing Kumbaya?"

"I haven't said anything because most of you don't know me." Ignoring Lynette's taunt, Claire walked over to Riley. "Riley isn't trying to get into your men's pants."

The phrasing sent a ripple of laughter through the room.

"We either trust her, and our men, or we don't. I trust mine. And I trust Riley. How about you?"

"I trust Sol. And Riley," Racine stated emphatically.

From there, it quickly snowballed until Lynette was the only one left who hadn't declared her support.

"Kyle doesn't screw around. Anymore."

Riley knew it was as close as the woman would get to jumping on the bandwagon. The important thing was, a potential crisis had been diverted and Riley had established some new friendships.

"Well done, Riley." Racine hugged her. "Wives and girlfriends have a lot of sway with their men. It never hurts to have them on your side."

"Something tells me when I'm running the team, these good feelings will be tempered during contract negotiations."

"No doubt." Racine laughed.

Her husband faced a new deal at the end of the season. However, that had little to do with Riley. In all likelihood, Sol would be retired before team ownership changed hands.

Riley believed their friendship would survive a contentious negotiation, but she was glad they wouldn't have to find out.

"That went well," Riley said when she and Claire headed home.

"Racine knew what she was doing. The women who attended will spread the word. *Riley Preston can be trusted with our men.*"

"God." Riley blew out a puff of air. "How did it come to this? I wouldn't know how to seduce all those men if I wanted to."

"Seduce? Riley, you're young and beautiful. Men are easy. With most of them, unintended eye contact is all it takes."

"I'm glad you didn't share that opinion today."

Claire grinned. "I had a great time. Good eats, plenty of juicy gossip, and some old-fashioned snark. Felt like a church social back in Iowa."

"I've never been to a church social."

Riley changed lanes. The freeway traffic was relatively mild. In an hour, it would be back to back commuters. Racine and Sol lived in Bellevue. The clever woman planned the get-together so anyone headed back to Seattle would miss the late afternoon bottleneck.

"I went for the food and left before anyone tried to save my soul."

"Was your soul in danger?" Riley enjoyed the stories Claire told about Iowa. She loved Seattle. However, she had always thought living in a small town would be nice. Claire made her rethink that. Neighbors who knew every intimate detail of your personal business? No, thank you.

"Compared to some of my friends, I was an angel. That didn't stop the true believers from trying to suck me in. I like my religion in small doses—if at all."

They rode in silence, happy with their own thoughts. Half an hour later, Riley pulled to a stop outside of Claire's apartment building.

"Thank you for speaking up for me," Riley said.

Claire patted her knee. "What are friends for?"

It was a good question. One that, until recently, Riley thought she knew the answer. However, thanks to Claire and Racine, the definition of friendship had taken on a wider scope.

It was nice to have someone to call up for lunch or a few drinks. This was deeper. Too often the word friend was thrown around with a casual ease. Riley hadn't realized how important a deep connection to another woman was.

Until now.

Chapter Thirteen

THE KNIGHTS LOST their second game of the season on a snowy night in Denver.

Road games were always tricky. Odd start times. Strange beds. Routines knocked out of whack. Then there was the wild card. The weather.

Riley watched the game from the comfort of her soft, comfy sofa. It was raining. A soggy, cold, early November afternoon. She hadn't felt like going out or having company. She ordered in beef barley soup and a side of garlic bread. Opened a can of diet root beer and snuggled under her favorite comforter.

She expected a win. She could have lived with a loss. Unfortunately, the game didn't simply slip away in the final minutes because of an iffy call by one of the officials. Kyle Trenton sustained a season-ending broken leg.

Riley didn't give a thought to her antagonistic encounter with Lynette. That had been a few weeks ago. A different time. A different situation. The woman's husband had been injured playing for Riley's team.

Rushing to her desk, she took out the player directory that contained everyone's home number.

Then she grabbed her phone and dialed.

"What?"

Under the bark, Riley could hear the tears in Lynette's voice.

"How are you, Lynette?"

"My husband is in a Denver hospital. He's over a thousand miles away and I can't get a flight out until tomorrow. How do you think I am?"

"Do you have someone who can stay with your children?"

"My mother is here."

"Good. Pack a bag. I'll send a car. By the time you get to the airport, there will be a private plane waiting to take you to Denver."

"Really?" The sound of Lynette blowing her nose made Riley wish she was there to hand her a tissue.

"You and Kyle are family. This is what we do."

"Thank you. I... Thank you."

"Have a safe flight."

Riley hung up. She had done everything she could. Kyle's treatment and recovery were out of her hands. However, if the Trenton family needed anything, she planned on making sure they got it.

IT FELT LIKE a typical Monday morning. The rain fell in cold, windy streaks against her bedroom window. All Riley wanted to do was stay in bed with Sean. Never mind their responsibilities.

From the moment Sean arrived at her door last evening, the rest of the world ceased to exist. Nothing could shatter their self-made cocoon unless they let it.

Almost nothing.

"I can't believe your father gave you grief."

"He blustered," Riley corrected, her head resting on Sean's shoulder. The mention of her father took a little shine off the morning "It's a company plane. I had every authority to use it. His only recourse was to emphasize, in rather a colorful use of language, how much he disapproved."

"Asshole."

Riley couldn't argue.

"He'll never change, Sean. You need to understand that."

"Are you warning me off?"

The laughter in his voice should have been a good thing. Riley sighed. Unfortunately, it meant Sean *didn't* understand.

Loving a man at a distance wasn't easy, but it had one advantage. Her parents weren't an issue when being with Sean had been a long shot. A dream she made herself stop believing would come true.

Now, he was a solid, honest-to-goodness part of her life. Which made Gerald and Corrine Preston a shadow she couldn't ignore. They were petty and vindictive. Eventually, some of it was bound to spill onto Sean.

The thought made Riley sick to her stomach.

"I wish you could have known my grandfather. He was the anti-Gerald."

"He loved you."

Riley nodded. "And showed me every day."

"I've heard stories. Coach Colman knew him. I can count on one hand the number of people Coach speaks about with reverence. Your grandfather is one of them."

"He made a deep impression on everyone."

Sean kissed her, loosening the knot in her stomach. She felt warm and safe. What they were building was good. Solid.

Maybe she made too much of her father's looming presence. Riley had the memory of her grandfather. Sean grew up with loving parents. She had to stop looking for trouble and simply enjoy precious moments like this one.

"Film." Sean kissed Riley's neck. "Study." His lips moved to her ear, his warm breath sending a shiver of sexual awareness through her body. "Work."

"None of those words make sense," Riley insisted. She slid her hand down his chest. "Kisses and erection? Only a big tease would start something he didn't intend to finish."

"You know me better than that."

It was slow. Mellow. Riley floated through a clear, warm sea of emotions. She lay back and let Sean spin a masterful combination of technique and natural ability around her body. The man loved what he was doing and it showed. No part of her was neglected.

It was a slow build. Riley clutched at the sheets, moaning Sean's name.

"God. When you call out to me, it sings in my blood. Say my name."

"Sean."

"Again." He kissed her. So sweet and undeniably erotic.

"Sean."

Riley sailed. She closed her eyes and swore that she was flying— over the edge into blissful oblivion.

Sean. My Sean.

"YOU NEED TO see this."

Sean sighed when Gaige passed him his phone.

"More pictures? It's been two weeks. I thought we were done with that shit."

"More like a lull before the next wave."

"I'd like to pulverize the person behind this. It isn't fair that most of this continually falls on Riley."

"Look at the picture, Sean."

The words that came out of his mouth were extreme—even for an NFL locker room.

"This is bullshit, Gaige."

"Okay."

"You don't believe me?" Incredulous, Sean advanced until he and his best friend stood toe to toe. "It. Is. Bullshit."

Sean was accustomed to seeing photographs of himself. In the United States, football was king. If a man played the game, he received a lot of attention. If that man played at a superstar level and looked like Sean, the attention was multiplied by a thousand.

As a young man, he craved the attention. Encouraged it. He dated the most beautiful women and frequented the hottest clubs because he knew it would add to his image as a player—on and off the field. Sean wasn't ashamed of his past. He'd had a damn good time.

However, he knew his reputation made the picture of himself and Ava Stanhope locked in a passionate embrace, harder to explain away.

"I haven't seen Ava in months. The last time, I was with Riley."

"I'm not accusing you, Sean." Gaige shook his head. "If you say it's an old picture, I believe you."

"Thank you."

"The world doesn't care if you screw every woman in sight. They love your playboy reputation. I wouldn't care. If you weren't dating Riley. She's the one who will have to deal with the blowback. Again."

"I need to get to her. Immediately."

Sean grabbed his jacket and was halfway out the door when Rob Cotter called out.

"I knew the choir boy routine was just an act, McBride. One woman is never enough for long."

When Sean stopped, his shoulders stiff, Gaige shoved him out the door.

"Go. I'll take care of that asshole."

When he was certain Sean was gone, Gaige slowly turned. His teammates recognized the steely glint in their QB's green eyes. One by one, they cleared the path, not wanting to get between him and Rob Cotter.

"You have a big mouth, Rob."

"Since when is McBride off limits to some harmless teasing?" Rob knew he had gone too far, but he wasn't willing to back down in front of the other Knights.

"See these?" Gaige held up his hands. Big. Strong. With long fingers and wide palms. Perfect for holding a football with ease—or doing serious damage to another man's face. "Tools of my trade. I can't afford to break a bone teaching you right from wrong."

"Jesus," Rob snorted. The bravado he tried so hard to cultivate was fading. Fast. "I'm not a rookie who needs Papa Gaige's sage advice."

"Then pull your head out of your ass, Cotter. Look around. Every man in this locker room is on a mission. A team. Moving as one, with the same goal. Why the hell are you determined to be the weak link? Why don't you want to win?"

"I do," Rob grumbled.

However, what Rob wanted—needed—even more, was money. He had a gambling habit, two ex-wives, and a career hanging by a thread, unraveling with every passing second. Maintaining a rah, rah attitude wasn't easy when he was surrounded by younger, more talented players. Gaige Benson and his buddy Sean McBride were on the top of Rob's shit list. Was it any wonder he took every opportunity to be a burr under their overpriced saddles?

"Here's my advice." Gaige looked him directly in the eye. "I suggest you take it. Riley Preston is off limits. Correction. All women are off limits."

"Excuse me? *All women*? What the hell does that mean?"

"Simple. You have a knack for saying the wrong thing about the wrong person. You never know who might be dating the woman you've singled out. Save yourself a fat lip. Keep your opinions, good or bad, to yourself."

"Locker rooms aren't supposed to be PC, Benson," Rob called out. Gaige was already out the door. Looking around for support, Rob found none. "Come on, guys. When did we become Boy Scouts? We're football players. That used to mean crude and rude."

"You heard Gaige. You can call him and Sean anything you want. Just lay off the ladies. Unless it's a Kardashian." Sol looked around. "Kardashians are safe. Right?"

"I kind of like Khloe," one of the guys called out.

"Really? Huh." Sol shrugged. "Well, there's no accounting for taste. Play it safe, Cotter. If it involves a woman, keep your thoughts to yourself, locked away inside that pea brain of yours."

Rob's temper spiked to a dangerous level. It wasn't easy to keep it tamped down until he was alone, but he managed it—barely. The inside of his truck took the brunt of his displeasure. A mile from the stadium he pulled over and proceeded to annihilate everything in sight.

Rob took a crazy kind of pleasure in destroying the seats, tearing at the upholstery until bits of foam padding littered the floor. The truck could be repossessed at any time. Unlike many of his teammates, no one gave him a slick ride to tool around in. He had to pay for it with his own hard earned money. He was a football player, Goddamn it. He shouldn't have to pay for anything. It was the dealership's fault. If they had given him the truck, they wouldn't have to worry about what it looked like. Rob ripped off the rearview mirror, smashing it to bits. Good luck reselling this baby.

Rob was in such a rage he almost missed the phone call. He was about to let it go to voicemail. Then he had a thought. Maybe it was one of his bitch ex-wives. He could kill two birds with one stone. Burn off some of his frustration, and put the bitch in her place.

"What now? Need more of my money?"

"No. I have plenty of my own."

Rob gripped the phone. Not an ex. Sweat from his exertions rolled down his face unnoticed. "Who the hell is this?"

"A friend."

"That's rich." Rob didn't have any friends. That scene in the locker room proved that.

"Would you like to be?"

"I don't know or care what you're talking about, asshole." Rob was about to hang up. His head hurt and he needed a drink—not riddles that made his already taxed brain hurt.

"Rich. Would you like to be?"

Slowly, Rob's thumb moved away from the keypad. He licked his lips.

"Who is this?"

"The man who can make all your money problems disappear. I can set you up on easy street for the rest of your life."

"Out of the goodness of your heart?"

The man laughed. "Nothing is free. It's up to you to decide how high a price you're willing to pay."

Rob could hear his mother's voice. *The devil lurks around every corner, Robert. Be strong. Be good. God will reward you in heaven.* Rob hadn't listened as a child and he wasn't listening now.

A life of ease and luxury? Hell yes. For that kind of guarantee, he would do anything the devil wanted, short of taking demonic cock up the ass. Rob laughed. Shit, he was desperate. At this point, he might consider a sulfur-infused sperm enema. If the payoff was big enough.

Eyes narrowed, Rob's thumb caressed the side of his phone.

"How much? And how soon can I get it?"

FINDING RILEY TURNED out to be easier said than done.

His calls went directly to voicemail. According to Stuart, the doorman at her building, she wasn't home and hadn't been all day.

Sean called Claire. His reception was chilly, her frosty voice almost freezing his ear. Because he knew she cared about Riley, Sean took the time to tell his side of the photograph. By the time he hung up, Claire seemed convinced of his innocence.

Riley's whereabouts was still a mystery.

He couldn't call her parents. They were the last people who would know what Riley was up to. Nor did he want to give them any ammo to use in future battles.

Gerald and Corrine Preston had spent most of Riley's life either ignoring her or throwing roadblocks in her path. They would have no interest in helping smooth over a bump in their daughter's personal life.

Sean was nearing panic mode. A woman with Riley's resources could be anywhere. Chicago. New York. Boston. Halfway to China. A passport and limitless money meant if Riley wanted to hide, his chances of finding her were not good.

Somewhere between beyond calculation and no fucking chance.

He leaned against his car, wondering what was going on in Riley's head. She'd seen the picture. Who hadn't? Right now, the social media world was having a field day. Football superstar plus supermodel plus owner's daughter equaled blogger's heaven.

Sean didn't care about the speculation. He cared about Riley.

Rubbing his face, he sighed. There was no point in mincing words. What he felt was way beyond caring or wanting. Lust? Definitely. However, a man didn't feel like this about a mere sex partner.

For the first time in his life, Sean McBride was in love. Head over heels, no coming back, until the end of time, love. And wonder of wonders? He didn't want to run.

Sean loved Riley.

Damn. Five years ago, who would have predicted that? The kid had grown up. And he wasn't talking about Riley. When it came to maturity, she had always been years ahead. Slowly, with a touch of reluctance, Sean had finally caught up.

Even a year ago, he hadn't been ready for her. Now that he was, would his wild past ruin his chances with the woman who had shown him what love was about?

"Excuse me? Mr. McBride?"

Sean turned. A small boy, maybe seven years old, stood at his side. His expression was a combination of excited and terrified. In one hand he held a pen, a white jersey in the other. In big black letters, McBride was sewn on the back.

"Hey." Sean pushed away his unhappy thoughts. Smiling, he crouched to the boy's level. "What do you have there?"

"I—Mom?"

"It's okay, Tad." She patted her son on the shoulder. "Ask Mr. McBride for his autograph."

"Tad? May I sign your jersey?"

With a shy nod, Tad handed him the shirt. Sean understood how much a moment like this meant to a boy. He grew up idolizing Jerry Rice. When they finally met, it was everything Sean hoped it would be.

Sean had a duty to the boy, and all his fans. It didn't matter what crap rained down on his personal life. It was up to him to make this moment something Tad would look back on with fondness for the rest of his life.

He spent five minutes pulling Tad out of his shell. When he and his mother walked away, they grinned from ear to ear. In addition to the autograph, Sean gave the boy a poster from the stash he always kept in his trunk. And promised to have tickets waiting at the box office next Sunday for Tad and his entire family.

Feeling a little better about the world in general, Sean used his phone to send his assistant a message about the tickets. That was the best five minutes he'd had since leaving Riley that morning.

Taking a deep breath, Sean was about to call her again when his phone rang.

"Claire. Any news?"

"She's at Providence Hospital. I'll text you the address."

"Hospital? What happened? Is she all right? Claire? *Claire!*"

Wild-eyed, Sean hit redial while fumbling with his keys. He had the car started before he realized Claire was not picking up.

"Fuck!" he yelled. Checking the address, Sean tossed his phone on the seat. A quick programming of his GPS and he shot out of the parking lot.

Was Claire on the way to the hospital and couldn't talk? Or was she trying to torture him, making his brain dream up the worst scenarios possible? Sean didn't care. He needed to get there as quickly as possible.

As it turned out, the hospital was surprisingly close. Sean ran a few stop signs without a thought of the consequences. For once, the streets were clear of traffic and police cars.

Briefly, Sean considered leaving his car at the emergency entrance but thought better of it. He found an empty parking spot that had just been vacated. He estimated the distance from here to the entrance to be about half a football field. Piece of cake. He was in the hospital in a flash. His breathing was normal, but his heart rate was through the roof with anxiety.

"I'm looking for Riley Preston."

"Do you know when she was admitted?"

"After nine this morning." Sean took a calming breath. It didn't work. "I can't—"

"Sean?"

His head whipped around at the sound of the wonderfully familiar voice.

"Riley. Thank God."

Sean pulled her into his arms. He might change his mind in an hour or two. But for right now, he never planned on letting go.

"What's wrong? Are you here to see Kyle?"

"Kyle?" Sean didn't let go. He spoke into her ear, taking in her soothing fragrance. "What the hell does he have to do with anything? Claire told me you were in the hospital."

"Because Kyle Trenton, your teammate, was transferred here from Denver earlier this afternoon. I came over to see how he was and to lend some support to Lynette."

"The next time I see Claire I will gleefully strangle her."

Still not himself, Sean let Riley lead him away from the front desk to a nearby waiting area. Gently, she pushed him onto a plastic chair.

"Why would Claire make you think I was in the hospital?"

"Pure spite." Sean held onto Riley's hand. He needed the connection.

"That doesn't sound like her. Unless—what did you do to her?"

"Nothing. I swear."

Gradually, Sean became aware of his surroundings. He and Riley were not alone. The waiting area was full and everyone was listening with unabashed interest.

Smiling at the gaping fans, Sean said under his breath, "We need some privacy."

"Come with me."

Riley took his hand. It was such a natural gesture. She couldn't be too pissed off if she didn't mind touching him.

"We can talk in here. Kyle is down getting x-rays and Lynette went with him."

The room was filled with flowers and balloons. Sean knew one of the arrangements was from him. He signed the card before practice. Another task his assistant took care of for him.

"How is he?"

"Great." Riley shrugged. "All things considered. He's upset about missing the rest of the season but his doctors see no reason he won't be back at full strength for training camp in July."

"That's a relief. Lynette and the kids? This must be tough on them."

"Lynette has a rod of pure steel in her spine. She was shaken. Now that the crisis has passed, she's taken over like a proper drill sergeant. I don't envy the hospital staff." Riley met his wary gaze. "You want to tell me what's going on? Or is there another bush you want to beat around?"

"Here."

Sean handed Riley his phone. He could stall like she said, or he could face it head on. God, stalling sounded good about now.

"Okay." Calmly, Riley looked up. "I give up. Why are you showing me a picture of you and Ava?"

"The article implies I slept with her on the team's last road trip."

"Did you?"

"No! Jesus, Riley."

"Because, yes, I would be upset." Riley took a deep breath. "But we haven't laid down any ground rules, Sean."

"What the hell does that mean?"

"Are we exclusive? Just you and me? No one else?"

"Of course!" Sean ran a distracted hand through his hair. Flecks of gold in his hazel eyes seemed to turn molten with emotion. "I don't want anyone else, Riley." A sickening thought occurred to him. "Do you?"

"No."

"Then I'm saying it. Straight out. No one else. I—" Something stopped him from saying he loved her. The setting? A hospital room wasn't the most romantic place to tell a woman something like that. Though there were roses. "I like what we have."

"So do I." Riley handed him the phone. "The idiot who is trying to stir up trouble needs to do a better job with their choice of pictures."

"I'm not a fan." Sean glanced at it again. "Everyone who has seen this has given me hell. Why didn't you?"

"Honestly." Riley shook her head. "Look closely, Sean. In the picture, your hair is, at least, three inches shorter than it is now. Unless you can magically grow it at a superhuman rate, that is obviously an old picture."

"Why didn't I notice that?"

Riley slid her arms around his waist. "Don't beat yourself up. I notice everything." She lightly kissed him. "You might want to remember that. For future reference."

"Mmm." Sean sank into the kiss, the tension that had built up for the last few hours draining away. "Thank you."

"For?"

"Not jumping to the obvious conclusion. I've learned today that it's hard to leave your reputation behind."

"You earned it honestly, Sean. One. Or two. Or three women at a time."

"You don't want to go there." Sean knew he was being teased. The weight was gone from his stomach—and his heart. So he had no problem teasing back. "The stories I could tell."

"Why don't we save those for another time. Far, far into the future."

Sean liked that idea. Not the part where he shared his sexual exploits. The part where they had a future. A long, long one.

"I'd like to see Kyle. Then, how about dinner?"

"Kiss me."

"Instead of dinner?"

Not waiting for an answer, Sean gladly took what she so sweetly offered. This kiss felt different. Deeper. More emotional. Sean wondered if she felt it. Did Riley understand that something elemental had changed inside him? Could she understand it was because of her?

Sean's arms tightened around her, pulling her close. Not long ago, the thought of spending the rest of his life with one person would have scared him to death. Now, his only fear was living a moment of his life without Riley.

Chapter Fourteen

"MY BODY IS saying thank you very much for the bye week." Sean nuzzled Riley's hair.

"And the rest of you?" Riley smiled.

"I hate to break our rhythm. We are running on all cylinders. I can't remember the last time I was on a team that felt this in tune with each other."

The music from the jukebox blanketed the bar in a mellow, bluesy atmosphere. The dance floor in the corner of the room wasn't meant for anything more than swaying in the arms of your partner.

That suited Riley and Sean just fine. There was no place they would rather be than in each other's arms. It didn't matter that they were surrounded by thirty plus Knights and their significant others. It felt as if they were in a world of their own.

"Coach Coleman wants you guys to forget about football for a few days."

"He knows that won't happen." Sean slid a hand through her silky hair, idly playing with the strands. "The best he can hope for is that no one will do anything stupid during his time off. Give an athlete a few days on his own, idiocy often ensues."

"I'm glad you have so much faith in your brothers."

"It isn't a lack of faith. It's years of experience."

"What is the stupidest thing you ever did?"

"Hmm. Are you asking as my girlfriend or my future boss?"

Riley pretended to think over the question. Any worries that her impending ownership of the Knights would be a sensitive subject dissipated long ago. It had never been about the team. It was the money. Once Sean wrapped his head around the concept of dating a very, very wealthy woman, it became a non-issue.

Sean was rich. So was she. The degree didn't matter.

"I'm your girlfriend."

Sean laughed. Most women would have jumped at the chance to hear one of his dirty little secrets. Not Riley. One reason to love her. The list grew daily.

"Yes, you are. And I'm your boyfriend."

"I like the sound of that."

"Me too."

Sean hadn't meant the kiss to be more than a sweet affirmation of their words. When it grew into something more, his mind wondered how soon he could get her back to his place. He loved Riley any way he could get her. However, naked Riley was his favorite.

"Break it up, you two. This is a respectable joint."

"Go away, Gaige." Blindly, Sean slapped in the general direction of his friend's voice.

"As captain and QB of the Knights, I am using my power to cut in. Go get a beer while I show the lady how a real man dances."

With a good-natured grumble, Sean transferred her into Gaige's arms.

"How does a real man dance?" she asked.

"With the grace of Fred Astaire and the cool of James Brown."

"That's quite a combo. You're setting yourself up for a big fall if you can't deliver, fella."

A twill, some fancy footwork, and an elaborate dip had the room applauding and Riley eating her words.

"Is there anything you can't do, you blond football God?"

"Calculus."

"Not exactly a fatal flaw."

Gaige settled them into an unhurried rhythm. Riley's dreams were coming true. A successful team. A thriving business. And Sean. First and foremost, Sean. She didn't know how many wishes she had left.

If she only had one, it would be for Gaige to find someone to love. He put on a damn good *I don't give a shit* face to the world. Riley knew better. He wanted what they all wanted.

That special someone to make the world a little less lonely.

"Let me set you up with—"

"No."

"When was the last time you went on an honest to goodness, dinner and a movie, date?"

"June sixth, two thousand five."

"That's specific," Riley laughed. "It must have been God-awful if you haven't done it since. Who was she?"

"The friend of a friend." Gaige's bright green eyes bore into her blue ones.

"Point taken."

They danced in the easy silence of good friends. Riley laughed to herself over the kooky Christmas decorations hung haphazardly around the bar. In spite of the name, *Overtime* didn't cater to the sports fan. It was a hole in the wall with a little buzz attached. Exactly how the owner wanted it.

Gaige frequented the place when he wanted low key and mellow. A Wednesday in early December was the perfect night to get a bunch of the team together for a private party. The closed sign was on the door. They were free to laugh and unwind without worrying about their pictures ending up on TMZ.

"Life is good?"

"No complaints."

"Except—?"

"I hate when you do that." Riley gave Gaige a playful punch on the shoulder. "Get out of my mind, Kreskin."

"You're too young to know who that is."

"So are you." With a sigh, she relented. "The poison pictures."

"They've stopped. There's no reason to think they'll start up again."

"We all know who was behind it, Gaige."

"Your father, and, or, your mother." Not a question. Bald, unadulterated fact.

"See? You didn't hesitate. For the rest of my life, I will have them hanging over me like a couple of demented swords of Damocles."

"Interesting analogy."

"And accurate."

Riley hated to bring up her parents. The ultimate buzzkill. She avoided the subject with Sean for that very reason. Why remind him of that less than stellar branch of her family tree.

"There isn't any proof, Riley," Gaige reminded her. His sympathy was tinged with reality. "You have to let it go."

"In a perfect world?"

"Go on. I'm all for one of those."

"Once the season is over, I would convene the board. After wowing them with my charm and eloquence, a unanimous vote would send my father packing."

"Followed by endless rainbows and dancing unicorns."

"You asked."

Gaige squeezed her hand. "In a not so perfect world?"

He had that, *I'm your friend, tell me your troubles*, look on his face. Riley caved every time.

"I would stop worrying about Sean waking up to fully realize what my family represents. Grandpa isn't around to temper the insanity, Gaige."

"No, but you are."

"Am I enough?"

Riley had few insecurities. Most of them centered around Sean.

"You, my dear, are a handful." Gaige dipped her again, bringing a smile to her face. "I think Sean is the man to take you on. *And* the baggage that comes with you."

157

Riley wished she was as certain as Gaige. By nature, relationships were never insular. The outside world would always want to chip away at the foundation. Riley could handle Sean's crazy fans and old lovers. He accepted that her money wasn't going anywhere.

Could she expect him to weather every storm her parents threw at them when each was bound to be crazier than the last? Was it fair to ask it of him?

"Enough about me. Tell me your problems."

Gaige had a great poker face. If Riley wasn't a good friend, she might have missed the hesitation—the slight shadow in his normally clear, green eyes.

"What could I have to complain about?"

Riley sighed. The shutter was back on the lens. Gaige kept his personal life close to the vest. Something troubled him, but he wasn't going to share it with her.

"I'm always here. You know. A sympathetic ear and all that stuff."

"I'll keep it in mind."

"Honestly?"

Gaige lightly kissed her cheek before whispering, "Honestly."

There wasn't anything else to say. She couldn't pull his problems from him. He was a rock for all of them. If the day came when he needed someone to lean on, Riley hoped he would finally let in the people who loved him.

Gaige gave her another quick kiss, then spun her into Sean's waiting arms.

"Hello, beautiful."

"Isn't that supposed to be my line?" Sean chuckled, his lips brushing her temple.

"I don't want us to play by anyone else's rules, Sean."

If they made their own rules, her family wouldn't matter. Riley knew it made no sense. However, if it helped banish her worries, even for a little while, that was all that mattered.

"Okay." Riley was grateful he didn't ask the question she could see in his eyes. "I like the idea of going our own way. The hell with what anyone else thinks."

"I'm with you."

Always, she thought, resting her head on his shoulder. And for tonight, she was content to sway in Sean's arms and shut out the rest of the world.

THERE WERE DAYS when the business world made her head want to explode. From sun up, to sun down, nothing went right. One thing piled onto another until she couldn't figure why she willingly put herself through the aggravation.

Then a day like today happened and it became clear. Riley would suffer a few headaches just to see the joy and excitement on Claire's face.

"Are those numbers real?"

"They are projections," Riley cautioned. Then, she grinned. "My staff is never off by more than a few percentiles. Write it down. Next Christmas, your line of balms and creams will be flying off the shelves."

They were in Riley's home office. As soon as the mock ups arrived, she had called Claire. The tall, leggy blonde looked fresh, well rested and at the moment, stunned.

Actually, she looked drunk. A little loopy. Riley doubted she could have walked a straight line without tipping over. Discovering all her hard work was finally going to pay off—in a big way—could stun the most grounded person.

Even someone as solid as Claire.

"I don't know what to say."

"Say you like the labels. Or don't. We have plenty of time to tweak them before Claire's Creations hits the market."

"The labels are great. I don't know how you did this so quickly."

"I delegated. The people who work for me deserve all the credit."

"If that were true, I would still be shopping my product around, hoping to find a manufacturer and distributor. Not to mention the worry of getting ripped off. I owe my lack of sleepless nights to you, Riley."

"I'm not doing this for nothing." Riley winked. "I expect to make a nice chunk of money off your toil and sweat."

"All of which you are donating to the Shriner's Hospital."

"It's a tax write-off."

"Stop!" Claire picked up her freshly delivered coffee. "Why won't you let me heap the praise where it's due?"

"Fine." Arms wide open, Riley sat back in her chair. "Heap away."

"You crack me up."

"Good to know. If everything goes south, I can always make a living as a comedian."

"Or a smartass." Claire paused. "Riley…"

"Do you have a problem with the label design?" Riley picked up a bottle of lemon-scented lotion. Their demographic was women. The line of men's products would roll out later next year. For now, they were concentrating on an upscale clientele with plenty of disposable income to spend. "Don't be afraid to speak up. It's your name on the product. You need to be one hundred percent happy."

"My name." Claire shrugged. "Do you think that's the way to go?"

"Ah, now I see. Face to face with success, my ultra-confident friend is morphing into a shrinking violet."

"No. I don't know. Maybe. Have you ever wanted something for so long you can't quite believe it's finally happening?"

Only every day—with Sean. Waking up next to the man she loved wasn't a dream. It was the best and brightest reality. She would never take it for granted. Though she couldn't get past the fear that it would suddenly be snatched away.

"You need to get used to your good fortune, Claire." Riley silently reminded herself of the same thing. "Enjoy it."

"That's what Logan keeps telling me." Claire looked at the ring shining on her left hand. "Not that he's one to talk. He doesn't say it, but I know he worries before every game that his knee isn't going to hold up."

"Is it that bad?"

Logan always appeared to be happy and carefree. On the football field, he played with complete abandon. Riley had no idea that he dealt with doubts.

"It's getting better every week. He didn't think he would ever play again. I can't blame him for being cautious. He was in a dark place when we met. Each game is a gift because he knows what it's like to have it taken away."

"That's the key, isn't it? You have to enjoy the moment instead of worrying about what might happen."

"Exactly."

It was good advice. And Riley planned on taking it to heart in her own life. Enjoy Sean—here and now.

"That's a nice smile," Claire said. "Want to share its source?"

"I'm happy."

"Me, too."

"Good." Riley snatched up her purse. "How about some lunch?"

"That Mexican place over on Hawthorne? My treat." Claire linked her arm with Riley's. "My business partner tells me that I can afford it."

Buoyed by their mutual good moods, they decided to walk to the restaurant. It was a sunny December day. Brisk but not freezing.

Riley and Claire turned a few heads. One tall and slender, the other more compact, with curves in all the right places. But it was their glowing faces that drew the most attention. Beauty, inside and out. It was an irresistible combination.

"Riley," a voice called out.

Hearing her name, Riley turned one way then the other.

"Over here!"

Riley didn't know what to call it. A whispered shout? Across the street, Sapphire stood in the shadowed doorway of a hardware store. She waved her arms, looked around furtively, then ducked out of sight.

"That's not the least bit odd," Claire frowned.

"Are we supposed to go over there?"

"Logan loves spy thrillers. I've watched so many I think I'm becoming paranoid." Claire glanced around for anyone in a trench coat. "If this were a movie, the smart thing would be to keep on moving. Shadowed figures never bode well for the protagonists."

"Riley!"

"I think we should take our chances." Still holding Claire's arm, she pulled her across the street. "But just in case, you keep a watch out."

"Laugh all you want. If a big black sedan comes barreling down the street, you'll be glad I had your back."

"What are you going to do? Pull out your Glock and shoot the tires?"

When Claire didn't answer, Riley stopped in her tracks.

"Are you carrying a gun?"

"No. Logan talked me out of getting a permit. I'm rethinking the decision. We had an ambush situation in Oklahoma."

"Rein it in, Annie Oakley. This is downtown Seattle. And that is Sapphire. I say we take our chances."

"Thank goodness. Come out of the light." Sapphire nervously licked her lips, her eyes darting from side to side. Normally put together from top to bottom, the woman looked frazzled. Not messy—but a bit of a mess. The buttons on her jacket were in the wrong holes and she was missing color on her upper lip.

Whatever was wrong, it had Sapphire off her game.

The doorway was a tight fit for three grown women, but Sapphire seemed determined not to move, so Riley went with it.

"What is going on?" Riley felt like a human sardine.

"I was afraid I wouldn't catch you in time."

"In time for what? Why didn't you simply call me instead of recreating a scene from *Three Days of the Condor*?"

"Oh, that was a good one," Claire nodded.

"I tried to call. It went to voicemail."

"Crap." Riley took out her phone. She turned it off when she plugged it in last night and forgot to turn it back on.

"I shouldn't be doing this." Sapphire moved farther into the shadows, her eyes darting toward the street. "But you were nice to me. Besides, this is wrong." From her bag, Sapphire pulled out a mini-iPod. "There's something you need to hear. I hope it isn't too late."

"Too late?" Riley's gaze met Claire's. That didn't sound good.

"Listen." Sapphire hit the play button.

She had no idea how long the recording lasted. A minute? An hour? As she listened to the voices plot the unthinkable, Riley felt first cold then unbearably hot.

"This has to be a joke," Claire exclaimed. "A sick, sick joke."

It wasn't a joke. It was her father. And he was deadly serious.

Without a word, Riley ran in the direction of the parking garage housed under her condo. Claire was at her side.

"Start making calls," she said, her voice unnaturally calm. "Anyone and everyone. Make them listen."

"Sapphire ran in the other direction."

"She warned us. I guess that was as far as her courage could carry her."

Riley didn't have time to worry about that. She was too busy staying upright and not breaking an ankle. For the first time in years, Riley cursed her four-inch heels. They slowed her down, but she didn't have time to take them off. She dialed as she ran.

No luck. She skipped Sean and Gaige. They wouldn't have their phones with them on the field. Wednesday meant everyone was at practice running full drills. There was no use wasting time trying to reach them directly.

"No one is answering." Claire's fingers were white where she gripped her phone.

"Keep trying."

Riley wanted to scream and kick and punch anything in her path. But now wasn't the time. She had to hold her emotions in check. If she started to cry, she might never stop.

Thirty feet from her car she used the remote to unlock the doors and start the engine.

"Where the hell is everybody?" No one answered at Knights' headquarters. "I've tried the front desk. The training room. Damn it. This can't be happening."

Riley's hand shook as she tried to insert the key into the ignition.

"Do you want me to drive?" Claire hesitated before buckling her seatbelt.

"No." On her third try, the key slipped in. "Just keep phoning. The building can't be deserted."

If they were lucky, they could get to the field in less than an hour. That would be pushing it. Praying for light traffic and no police cars, Riley sped around the corner. She heard Claire leaving messages. So far she had reached nothing but voicemail.

"Finally." Claire pumped her fist. "I have the head of maintenance. He can get security."

"No. That's perfect. Put him on speakerphone." Riley's heart was in her throat. She swallowed, trying to make room for her words.

"Deacon? This is Riley Preston."

"Riley? Is that panic I hear in your voice? Tell me what you need."

Thank God. She had known Deacon Michaels when he cleaned floors at an hourly wage. He would turn a blind eye to her slinking around the stadium—always making sure she stayed safe. Now he was top man and exactly the person Riley needed.

"I don't have time to explain, Deacon."

"Then stop talking and tell me what's up."

"I need you. And every man you can get your hands on."

Riley merged into traffic saying a silent prayer. Please, don't let them be too late.

"THAT LAST PLAY looked like shit. Where the hell are your heads? You think Miami is going to roll over and let us stroll into the end zone just because we have a better record?"

Harry Coleman stopped in front of a big rookie offensive lineman. Without a word, he had the younger man fidgeting from side to side.

"He did the same thing to me when I was a rookie." Logan shook his head. "I got *the look* in training camp. I sweated bullets, convinced he was going to cut me."

"He singles a newbie out every year," Gaige said with a chuckle. "Pretty boy here almost lost his lunch when his turn came."

"I was green around the gills for a month," Sean agreed. It was easy to smile now. Eight years ago, he couldn't find any humor in it.

They were on the practice field and things weren't going well. Normally sure-handed receivers dropped passes. Running backs acted as though the ball was covered in grease. *Ha. Good one. Greased pig skin.* Wisely, Sean kept the joke to himself.

The offensive line had more holes in it than swiss cheese. If there were ever a time for Harry to pull out his patented rookie mind-screw, this was it.

"And you." Harry turned on Rob Cotter.

"What did I do?" Rob's eyes darted around the field, landing on anything but the coach. "I've been playing hard all practice."

"Too hard. Those are our guys on the other side, Cotter. Pull up before you do some damage. Understood?"

"I can't help it if the offensive line isn't doing their jobs."

"Are you arguing with me?"

"No, Coach." Rob wiped the sweat from his upper lip. He'd taken something before practice. A pill meant to chill his nerves. It seemed to be having the opposite effect. "You're the boss."

"Damn straight." Impossible as it seemed, the volume of his voice rose. "That seven and two record doesn't mean shit. Miami will be gunning for us. Do you understand?"

"Yes, Coach," the team chanted as one.

"If I get the impression a single one of you is looking past Sunday, I will ream you a new one." He got in the rookie's face. "You want to walk around with two assholes?"

"No, sir."

"I love that man." Sean whispered the words, but the men standing next to him heard and agreed wholeheartedly.

"What the hell?" Harry's attention shifted to the end of the stadium. "Get off my field. Now!"

Puzzled, Sean turned. Close to a dozen men ran toward them at full speed. They wore jackets in the team colors, the blue and gold signaling that they worked for the Knights. However, they didn't belong on the field in the middle of practice.

"Sorry, Coach." Deacon Michaels faced Harry Coleman without an ounce of visible fear. His burly arms were crossed, his feet planted a shoulder's width apart. Behind him, the other men mimicked the stance. "We have our orders. No one makes another move until Ms. Preston gets here."

Riley? Sean shrugged when everyone looked his way. He was as puzzled as they were.

"Deacon, right?"

"Yes, sir."

"Deacon, Ms. Preston doesn't have the authority to interrupt my team during practice. Get your asses out of here right now and maybe, *maybe*, you'll keep your jobs. In ten seconds, I won't give you any guarantees."

"With all due respect, Coach."

"Don't say it," Harry warned.

"We aren't budging."

Sean worried that Harry was on the brink of blowing something vital. The red face, the bugged-out eyes. The steam coming out of his ears. None of that boded well for Harry's health.

"We'll take care of them, Coach." Rob Cotter and five massive linemen stepped forward.

"You." Deacon pointed. "Ms. Preston told me to keep a close eye on you."

Rob swallowed, but backed by his teammates, he held his ground.

"Stand down." No one made a noise, yet Harry's voice was getting louder. "Do you want to break your hand three days before the next game?"

"No. The idea was to break Sean's leg."

Out of breath, a pair of high-heeled boots in one hand and gripping her phone with the other, Riley ran to Harry—but her eyes were on Sean. Close behind, Claire stopped beside Logan. Seeing the questions in his eyes, she shook her head, then she took his hand and squeezed.

"You want to explain?" Harry growled.

"Are you okay?" Riley asked Sean.

"I'm fine. What about you?" Dropping his helmet, Sean took Riley into his arms.

"Great. Now." Riley's arms circled his waist, never wanting to let go. She didn't care about the sweaty uniform or bulky pads. Sean was in one piece. Thank God.

"This is sweet." Harry's words dripped with sarcasm and heat. "You've disrupted practice and if I'm not mistaken, accused one of my players of something heinous. You'd better start explaining."

"Not here." Reluctantly, Riley let Sean go. "Please, Harry. The damage is already done. Give me ten minutes. If you don't agree that I did the right thing, I'll let you ban me from the stadium. Permanently."

That was enough for Harry. He knew two things about Riley. One. She didn't go around crying wolf. And two. She loved the Knights too much to risk being banned. Whatever was happening, it was serious.

"Well, I'm not standing around for this shit. If practice is over, I going home." Rob Cotter blustered.

"You leave the stadium, you're off the team." Harry pinned Rob with his steely gaze. "That goes for everyone. Hit the showers, but stick around."

"This is your rodeo," Harry said to Riley. "Who do you need?"

"You, Sean, and Gaige."

"Come on. Let's go to my office."

Chapter Fifteen

"SHOULD I BRING everyone some coffee?"

"This isn't a social call," Harry barked at his secretary.

Used to his ways, the woman didn't blink an eye or miss a beat. Without looking up, she continued rapidly typing away.

"Should we call your father in on this?"

"Believe me, he already knows."

Riley waited until the men were seated. Deciding to let the recording do the talking, she silently pulled the iPod out of her purse and hit play. The voices were instantly recognizable. Gerald Preston. And Rob Cotter.

"You've been betting on games."

"Never on the Knights."

"Son of a bitch." Stunned, Gaige shook his head.

"You think that matters?" Gerald laughed. "Ask Pete Rose how that defense worked for him. You won't play another down if word of this leaks."

"I was done after this season. What difference does it make?"

"Reputation can earn you a few bucks after you retire. Yours will be shot. However. Do me a little favor and you'll get out of this without the stink of a cheater."

"Fuck that. You mentioned money. Lots of it."

There was a pause. Riley could almost see her father's sly smile.

"Five million. In an untraceable offshore account."

"Who do I have to kill?" Rob laughed.

"Not murder. Simply mayhem. Break Sean McBride's leg. Or arm. Pick a bone. As long as it takes him out for the rest of the season. I'll throw in two million if the injury ends his career."

Riley couldn't look at Sean. She felt too sick and ashamed.

"How am I supposed to pull this off?"

"Things happen during practice. Blindside him. No one will call it anything but an unfortunate accident."

"They might call it deliberate."

"Who cares. The Knights won't win squat without McBride. You can sit at home on your pile of money and watch them flame out in the first round of the playoffs."

This time, it was Rob who paused. For a heartbeat.

"I get to teach McBride a long overdue lesson and get paid for it? Consider it done."

Stunned didn't begin to describe the silence that filled the room. Thick and oppressive, Riley closed her eyes and waited for the inevitable barge.

"Where did you get that." Unlike on the field, Harry's voice held no emotion.

Not what she had expected, but it was as good a first question as any.

"My…" Riley couldn't bring herself to call him her father. "Gerald's assistant. It seems he's been playing Richard Nixon. Every conversation in his office is recorded. She took a big chance, getting me the recording."

"I'm flummoxed." Harry sighed. "What's our move? Turn the recording over to the police?"

"Tempting. But no." Between panic and nausea, the drive to the stadium had given Riley time to think. "If everyone agrees, I say we handle it internally. That means keeping this between the four of us. Five if you count Claire. Make that six."

"Logan," Gaige nodded. "Okay. I get where you're going. I agree.

The team doesn't need the kind of media circus this story would create. However, Gerald and Rob can't walk away scot free. What they planned is unconscionable."

"I agree. What should we do?"

"Sean?"

"Hmm?" Shaking away the haze of disbelief, Sean looked at Gaige. "What?"

"Your career was at stake. What do you want to do?"

"Burn the bastards." Sean slammed his fist onto the arm of his chair, rattling the frame. "What the hell? Why?"

"You know the answer."

"Riley." Sean held out his hand. "Please."

She was too tired to argue. The adrenaline surge that had gotten this far was dropping fast. Riley dropped into the seat next to Sean.

"I don't have any answers. Except this. We all know why you were targeted. If all he wanted to do was derail the Knights, why not take out Gaige?"

"Because Gerald wanted to hurt you *and* the team." Sean didn't like how cold her hand was. He rubbed it between his, hoping to provide some heat. "He's a bastard. We've always known that."

"This reaches a different level." Gaige patted Riley's back. His mind was working a mile a minute, trying to figure out a solution to this mess.

"Here is my suggestion. Tell the team it was an outside threat. Cut Rob. Use the recording as leverage. Hopefully, he'll be smart enough to slither into a very deep hole and keep his mouth shut."

"What about…"

"My father?" Riley's tried to smile, but her lips wouldn't cooperate. "We can't avoid calling him what he is Sean. He's my father. And he's my problem."

"What does that mean?" Sean stood when she did.

"It means the three of you have a game to get ready for."

"And you?" Gaige asked.

Riley paused by the door. Without turning, she said, "I'm going to dropkick his ass as far as humanly possible."

"Tell me you'll be okay?"

Sean had followed her into the corridor. He looked as wiped out as she felt.

"This has been coming for a long time. It never occurred to me it would come to a head in such a dramatic manner." Unable to stand it a moment longer, Riley rushed into Sean's arms. "Thank God you're all right."

"My hero."

"Are you laughing?" Riley couldn't believe her ears.

"It's either laugh or cry. It isn't manly to cry." Tipping her chin, Sean looked into her eyes. "I'm standing, Riley. We both are. Do you know what that means?"

"Tell me. I need some good news."

His lips brushing hers, Sean whispered the answer.

"We won."

IT TOOK TWO days to track down her father.

Not that he was hiding. Exactly. The Caribbean island retreat wasn't a secret to anyone. Access was by boat or helicopter, making it difficult for the average person to get there, however, Riley was not your average person. She had the resources to travel any place in the world with little or no notice.

Riley stepped onto the dock, rolling her head from side to side, trying to loosen the knots. They weren't the result of long hours on a private jet or the luxury yacht ride from the main island. The knots had formed two days ago when she heard the recording of her father plotting to remove Sean from football—permanently. She hadn't relaxed, or slept, since.

Riley hoped today's meeting would go a long way toward righting her current state of perpetual anxiety.

"He knows we're here." Ross Morrisey nodded toward the security camera mounted above the dock.

"He knew before we arrived. This isn't about him hiding. It's another one of his games."

Calling Ross Morrisey had been Riley's first move after she left Knights' headquarters. As the senior member of the board and her friend, it made sense to let him know what was going on.

Ross agreed to her plan. Keeping as many details as possible out of the press was goal number one. The statement needed to be straightforward and convoluted, all at the same time.

After years of exemplary service, Gerald Preston is stepping down as president of the Knights, effective immediately. The Knights' organization is pleased to announce that long-time minority owner Ross Morrisey has agreed to step into the job. Everyone expects it to be a seamless transition.

Blah, blah, blah.

Riley approved the message. It was up to the PR department to field calls and sell the message. Her job was to make what was going on behind the scenes stay there. If her father wanted to draw out the drama, so be it. No matter where this meeting occurred, the end result would be the same.

"Running to his little hidey-hole is immature beyond words." Ross wiped the perspiration from his forehead. He was an active, fit man. However, the quick transition from cold, rainy Seattle to the eighty-plus weather was a shock to his system.

"Why aren't you sweating?" Ross looked closely at Riley's face. "Dry as a bone."

It was hard to sweat when your insides were coated with ice. Riley wondered if she would ever be warm again. Then she saw her father lounging on his ocean view veranda—a tropical drink in one hand, a cigar in the other—and the heat that had eluded her for two days shot through her veins.

It appeared the bastard didn't have a care in the world. In all likelihood, he didn't. To feel anything approaching guilt or remorse, you needed a conscience—something her father never had, and never would.

"Welcome to paradise. You've had a long flight. Sit. Have a drink."

"Are you fucking kidding me?" Mouth agape, Ross looked at Gerald, then at Riley. "He's crazy. Right?"

"No."

It was all part of the game. This time, Riley wasn't playing.

"Sign the papers." She dropped the document onto her father's lap.

"Hello to you, too." Gerald took a puff from his cigar. His crisp white shirt and perfectly pressed linen slacks looked as cool and unruffled as he did.

Riley didn't blink.

"What? No moral outrage? No recriminations? I'm disappointed, Riley."

"Sign the papers."

"Don't you want to know why I did it?"

"I do." Ross took a bottle of water from the umbrella-covered drink station, chugging the contents.

"I already know."

"You do?"

Gerald and Ross asked the question simultaneously. Ross incredulous. Gerald skeptical.

"Daddy issues."

Riley had the satisfaction of seeing her father's cool slip. That little tick in the corner of his eye made the trip worth every mile.

"You can't be serious?" Ross paused in the middle of opening another water. "That's—"

"Sad and pathetic?" Riley watched Gerald's grip on his cigar tighten. "I agree."

"You don't know what you're talking about."

The cigar snapped. Riley didn't think he noticed.

"Grandpa didn't love you enough. He loved me too much. That has been the basis of our relationship since day one."

"Sounds like someone is quoting her shrink."

"I didn't need to lie on a couch to figure that one out."

"Good for you." Gerald picked up the document. "Should I have my lawyer look these over?"

"I would."

That was all it took. Without glancing at the contents, Gerald picked up a pen and signed away his rights to the Seattle Knights. God, Riley thought with amazement. Her father, for all his intelligence and business acumen, was woefully predictable.

"Are we done?" Gerald held out the papers.

"Yes. I believe we are."

"HERE'S TO TEN and two. Let's celebrate tonight. Tomorrow it's back to reality."

Sean raised his bottle to Gaige's toast. As Harry predicted, Miami hadn't rolled over. The game had been a hard fought affair, but the good guys had come out on top. The team had put aside the drama of the last few days—banding together. On and off the field.

The Rob Cotter issue wasn't discussed. Sean wasn't certain if his teammates bought that the guy was cut—end of story. If there were any questions, no one asked them.

Instead of heading off in different directions as they usually did after a long flight home, most of the guys gathered at *The Extra Point*. Some played pool. Some sat around and rehashed the game. It was all about supporting each other—through thick and thin.

"I'm proud of you." Gaige clicked his beer bottle against Sean's. "You played a hell of a game. It couldn't have been easy with all that's on your mind."

"Between the lines, brother. Sometimes I think that game time is the only sane place left on Earth."

"Sad but true." Gaige leaned back in his chair. "Have you heard from Riley?"

"Three texts and a quick call before she left town."

For all intents and purposes, Riley had been incommunicado since Wednesday afternoon. She explained what she needed to do. He understood that it was difficult and she didn't have time to be in constant contact. That didn't stop him from worrying. This mess had hit her hard. Harder than anyone realized.

The world saw a strong, confident woman. And that's exactly what she was. She was also human. Sean wished he was with her to lend some moral support. He wished she would call him and let him know she was all right.

"She's due back tonight."

"How do you know that?" Sean demanded. And why the hell didn't he?

"She wanted to know where you were." Gaige showed him the text.

"Why not contact me directly?"

"Ask her yourself."

Sean's head whipped around. Riley stood at the door looking fresh as the proverbial daisy. She wore a red leather jacket and jeans. Casual. Elegant. Just like Riley.

Eyes fixed on the most beautiful sight in the world, Sean weaved his way through the crowd.

"You look tired."

Riley smiled. "So do you."

"I'm beat."

"Me, too."

Sean wrapped his arms around Riley's waist and lifted her off the ground.

"Hey, Sol."

"Yeah?"

"Open the door."

With a sigh, Riley rested her head on Sean's shoulder. No one said a word or tried to stop them. The team simply smiled and watched as he carried her out of the bar.

SEAN'S BEDROOM WAS blissfully quiet. His steady breathing was the only sound. He had fallen asleep moments after making love to her. And that's what he'd done. Made love. Riley had felt it in the way he slowly undressed her. His gentle touches and lingering kisses. Sean made her feel cherished. She knew he loved her. As much as she loved him.

It made leaving him the hardest thing she would ever do. She had made the decision before she met with her father. She wasn't good for him. Because of her, he almost lost his career. The thought of Sean, crippled for life, was all the extra push Riley needed. This relationship was poison for him.

Desperately, she wanted to hold on. Loving him meant she had to let him go.

Riley slipped from the bed. She felt around for her clothing Shirt. Jeans. Boots. She couldn't find her panties. Sean turned but didn't wake up. Afraid to wait any longer, she tiptoed from the room.

A note wasn't the smoothest way to end it. But Riley didn't care. It was her way. She set the folded paper where she knew Sean would find it. Entering the elevator, she waited for the doors to close. Then, alone, unable to hold back any longer, she sank to the floor and cried.

Chapter Sixteen

A FUCKING NOTE!

Sean didn't linger in the shower. He was pissed. Not angry. He reserved the right to that emotion after he found Riley and received a reasonable explanation. Not that there was one. He loved her. He knew damn well she loved him. The rest didn't matter.

Sean blindly gathered something to wear, his wet hair leaving damp spots on the t-shirt as he pulled it over his head. This was about her father. And her mother. The be all and end all examples of parental dysfunction. With the love of her grandfather and a whole lot of strength, Riley managed to become a woman to be admired. When he found her, he planned on reminding her of that. After he kissed the breath out of her. And possibly added a swat or two on her ass.

When we see each other, it will be as if it, we, never happened.

It happened, all right. Every second. Every minute. Every hour. Every day of the past eight years. As far as Sean was concerned, all of it counted. From the moment they met. Through Riley's crush. Through his wild ways. It led to now. He wasn't letting her throw it away.

First, he had to figure out where she was. Grabbing his phone, Sean began dialing.

"Hello?" Claire's greeting was slurred.

"It's six fucking thirty. Tell Sean to stick whatever it is up his ass and fuck off." Logan's words were clear as a bell.

"You said it for me, love of my life."

Sean didn't have time for Claire and Logan's routine. "Where is Riley?"

"You mean you lost her again. Bad form, Sean."

"This isn't a joke."

"Okay. What did you do?"

"Nothing."

"Right."

"This time, I swear, it wasn't me."

"I'm taking your word for it. But if I find out differently…"

"You can kick my ass."

"Last time I saw her, the two of you were leaving the bar."

"I need to call Gaige."

"Sean." Claire stopped him before he could hang up. "Let me know when you find her."

"I will."

Sean grabbed his jacket. If he had to, he would check every coffee shop in the city. Riley was bound to hit one of them. Unless she left town. Shit. Last time she ran, she told Gaige. Hoping she stayed true to form, Sean hit the elevator button and Gaige's number at the same time.

"Early," Gaige growled.

"So I've been told."

"Fuck off."

"I've heard that one, too. I'm looking for Riley."

"As in, I have no idea where she is? Because I don't like the sound of that."

The elevator door opened. There, looking small and utterly defeated, sat Riley.

"Sean? Is Riley okay?"

"False alarm."

Sean tossed the phone on the table. Taking two long steps, he bent down and picked Riley up.

"You're cold as ice."

"I'm an idiot." Riley hiccuped. "I couldn't do it, Sean. I meant to leave. I really did."

"But you didn't." Sean headed to the bedroom. Carefully, he set Riley onto the bed, removed her shoes then his, and joined her under the covers. "That makes you anything but an idiot."

"I love you."

"Again. Not an idiot." Sean tucked Riley close, his arm pillowing her head. "You've been crying." He kissed each tearstained cheek. "Did it make you feel better?"

"No. Maybe." Riley snuggled closer to his warm body. "I was filled with righteous good intentions when I got on the elevator. They lasted about ten seconds."

"How long were you in there?"

"I have no idea."

"Riley?"

"Yes?"

"I love you."

If she had a single tear left, Riley would have shed them. Instead, she looked at Sean and asked, "Why?"

"Why not?"

"I have two very good reasons."

"Here's the thing. You have a crazy family."

"To put it mildly."

"My family is just as crazy, but in a good way."

"How crazy? And how good?"

"I'll give you the perfect example." Sean reached around her to open the end table drawer. "Last week when I was speaking with my mother, I told her how good things were going between us."

"Okay."

"The next day this arrived."

Sean held up a ring. A diamond ring.

"That's…"

"The woman sent me my grandmother's engagement ring. For you. After I mentioned you two, maybe three times. Crazy, right?"

"Yes. And incredibly sweet."

"I thought so too." Without asking, Sean slipped it on her finger. "Look at that. A perfect fit. It isn't very big."

"It's perfect." Riley sighed. So much for trying to get away. Sean was stuck with her now. "I want to get married right after the season."

"Good. This engagement has gone on long enough."

"What? A whole two minutes?"

"Eight years, Riley. Eight unbelievable years."

Epilogue

SEAN WAS RIGHT. His family was crazy. In the best possible way. His mother decided she couldn't wait another day to meet Riley.

Sean tried to talk her out of coming, but there was no stopping Susan McBride. Her baby was engaged. And since Sean couldn't leave Seattle, they would come to him.

"I'm sorry. If I'd known she would do this, I would have waited to tell them."

Riley was at the airport, a slightly anxious greeting party of one. The practice was running late so he couldn't make it.

"It will be fine." She told him, hoping Sean couldn't hear her nerves through the phone. "I love that your mother is excited. I'm letting mine read about it online."

"That works for me."

Corrine Preston was currently wintering in Hawaii. Gerald was still in the Caribbean. They would return to Seattle. It was inevitable. However, Riley didn't care. For years, the only thing they had in common was the Knights. Without that, she couldn't envision a single scenario that would compel her to have anything to do with either of them. And she was fine with that. More than fine. She was ecstatic.

She had Sean. Riley glanced at her ring finger and grinned.

Sean. Their friends. The Knights. And his big, crazy family. After all these years. After thinking it would never happen. Riley had it all. And she was never letting it go.

How to Get in Touch

Please visit me at these sites, sign up for my newsletter, or leave a message.

http://www.maryjwilliams.net/home.html

https://www.facebook.com/Mary-J-Williams-1561851657385417

https://twitter.com/maryjwilliams05

https://www.pinterest.com/maryj0675/

https://www.goodreads.com/author/show/5648619.Mary_J_Williams

More Books by
Mary J. Williams

Harper Falls Series
If I Loved You
If Tomorrow Never Comes
If You Only Knew
If I Had You (Christmas in Harper Falls)

Hollywood Legends Series
Dreaming With a Broken Heart
Dreaming With My Eyes Wide Open
Dreaming Of Your Love (Coming in May)
Dreaming Again (Coming in July)
Dreaming of a White Christmas (Coming in December)

One Pass Away
After The Rain
After The Fire (Coming in June)